# THE DEAD HOUSE

Other  titles

# anne cassidy
# THE DEAD HOUSE

Hodder
Children's
Books

a division of Hachette Children's Books

ISBN-13: 978 0 340 93228 5

Typeset in Baskerville by Avon DataSet Ltd,
Bidford-on-Avon, Warwickshire

Printed in the UK by CPI Bookmarque, Croydon, CR0 4TD

The paper and board used in this paperback by Hodder Children's
Books are natural recyclable products made from wood grown
in sustainable forests. The manufacturing processes conform to the
environmental regulations of the country of origin.

Hodder Children's Books
a division of Hachette Children's Books
338 Euston Road, London NW1 3BH
An Hachette Livre UK company

# Part One

# House of Ghosts

# 1

Lauren went to look at the house late at night. The street was dark and wet, the rain falling in a warm drizzle. She had a jacket on even though it was too hot. It was buttoned up to the neck and the collar was up as though she was trying to hide inside it. She walked up and down the street for a while her eyes seeking out the houses until she finally saw it. Number 49.

She stared at it. She held her breath for a second expecting something to happen inside her. Some sense of recognition; goosebumps or her heart racing. But there was nothing. It was just a house, no different from the ones on either side, or those in the terrace opposite.

She backed into the shadow of a hedgerow and looked across at the building. The darkness had diluted its colours and smudged its shape. Her eyes travelled up and down anyway, trying to find a point of memory. At the top was the attic window. She must have looked out of it when she'd lived there. As a small child the height must have scared her. Looking down onto the street and seeing cars go by and people walking past. Such a long way down. So far to fall. Had she ever wondered that?

There were lights on in the big bay window on the

ground floor. A couple of shapes walked back and forth. The people who lived there. Jessica told her that many people had lived there over the last ten years. A builder had bought it and converted it into three flats letting them for short periods of time. Lauren wondered about all the tenants who had had the middle flat. Had they known the truth of the house? Had anyone ever told them?

A car pulled up along the street. It looked like a taxi or mini cab. Its headlights sent out a beam and she could see the rain falling across it, soft and thin like muslin. There was music playing inside the car and someone was in the back, behind the driver, talking. She looked back to the house. A light had gone on in the first floor front window. It wasn't a separate flat any more, she knew that. A family had bought the house and were restoring it to the way it used to be. Jessica had told her this before they left Cornwall. *You won't mind that we'll be living so close?* she'd said and Lauren had spent time reassuring her. *I don't care. It was ten years ago. I was only seven. I've had a whole lifetime since then.*

And she had. For ten years she'd lived with Jessica, her mum's sister, and Donny, Jessica's boyfriend. Just the three of them. Most of that time they'd lived in a house just outside St Agnes, a costal village on the north Cornish coast. It was as different from London as it could be. Acres of sky and sea and the sound of water a constant backdrop. In London there wasn't much sky, just endless brick walls and the moving panoply of cars and lorries. Grey, grey and more grey. Not something she would have noticed much under seven years of age. Then her life was full of other things; her mum, her sister Daisy, her toys, her school friends. Much of this had faded in her mind; like an old photograph, the colours were no longer bright, the edges had curled, the faces seemed like strangers.

The car door opened and the music tumbled out into the street. A lad got out of the car and said something to the driver. Then he stood up straight, closed the door and patted the roof of the car. He stayed in the rain as the car drove away. Lauren heard the splash as the wheels went through a puddle. She stared at him. He was thin and tall with dark curly hair. He was carrying a big rucksack on one shoulder and on the pavement was a hold-all. There were labels around the handles as if he'd just come off a plane. Her eyes travelled back up to his face and she saw that he was looking straight at her. It startled her. She'd thought she was hidden. But he looked away immediately so maybe she was mistaken. She took a small step backwards, feeling the prickly hedgerow at her back.

He went up to the house. Number 49. The door was already open by the time he got there, a rectangle of light falling onto the pathway. There was a shriek of delight and a woman appeared with her arms out. Lauren couldn't hear the words spoken but the tone was light and fluttery. Then the front door closed, slicing the light off, and the street was dark again.

Lauren felt as if she'd been shut out.

Why had she come here? Had it been because of the Art assignment?

The lesson they had had that afternoon had been about the summer Art exam. The theme was *The Child in Play*. They had started brainstorming about childhood games and pastimes. They each had to draw a sketch linked to the theme. At the end of the session the teacher had asked them all to pin these at random angles on a free-standing display board. When it was done Lauren stood back and looked. Amid the drawings of trains and dolls and teddy bears was a single image of a clown. It caught her eye and she scrutinised it. It stood out awkwardly. As though it belonged to another theme entirely She let her eye slip down and saw her own drawing. A doll's house. Tiny figures in a room of miniature furniture. By the side was a giant eye looking at it.

Of course she thought of her childhood home in Hazelwood Road. How could she not?

Now she looked at the closed door and imagined what was going on inside at that moment. A much-loved son returning from a holiday or maybe a trip abroad. A family waiting for him. A bottle of wine or even champagne ready to be opened. A celebration; a family reunited. Maybe it was the son's first sight of the house. Jessica said it had only been bought at auction in the previous six months. Maybe the son was standing in the hallway at that very moment, looking round, admiring the shape of the place. High ceilings! Mosaic floor! Original banisters!

A picture formed in her head, blurry. She was a child, sitting on the stairs, halfway up, halfway down. Her knees were poking out from under her dress, small and bony, her legs as thin as sticks. Her mum was in the hallway. Beside her were Jessica and Donny. Both had bags on the floor which had travel labels on the handles like tiny flags. Her mum was kissing Jessica and patting Donny's shoulder. *Are you sure you'll be all right?* Jessica was saying. *'Course we will,* her mum answered. *You could have come with us. It's only two hours' flying time to Spain!* Jessica said. Her mum shook her head and said, *You get off. You don't want to miss your plane.* There was a hall mirror behind her mum and Lauren could see the reflection of the three of them. For a second it looked as though there were six people in the hallway. *'Bye Lolly!* Jessica shouted as they went out of the door. *Her name's Lauren,* her mum said, tutting, pretending to be annoyed. Then the picture changed. Lauren wasn't wearing a dress but sitting on the stairs in her pyjamas. Daisy was crying upstairs but her mum wasn't taking any notice. She was standing at the front door pushing the bolt across, turning the key in the lock, fixing the chain. She was mumbling things that Lauren couldn't quite hear and all the time Daisy was crying. When she turned round her face was serious. *We're safe now,* she said. What happened next? Lauren couldn't remember. The picture in her head faded, the edges of it becoming frothy, dissolving. Memories were like the sea, coming closer, moving away, impossible to grasp, to hold on to.

Her mobile sounded. The ring tone was soft like a tinkling piano. She pulled it out of her pocket. The name

*Donny* was there. She considered answering it but didn't. Donny probably wanted to check up on Jessica, to see if she had stopped crying. To see if she was calm enough for him to return to the house, to pick up his things. Lauren sighed and wondered what to do. It was almost eleven. Jessica might be worried about her. On the other hand she might be so obsessed with the loss of Donny that she hadn't even noticed Lauren's absence. A beep sounded. Donny had sent a text. If he couldn't reach her in one way he'd do it in another. She read the message. It was just what she'd expected. Full of exclamation marks and abbreviations. He was sorry but things change, people change etc, etc, Love Donny.

They'd moved away from Cornwall because Donny, who was a Maths teacher, had got a new job in a school in East London. It was a promotion and tons more money and Donny said that they could use their house in Cornwall as a holiday home, an escape when they'd had too much of the city. They'd rented a small house in Bethnal Green and Jessica was looking for a job.

The move had come at a good time. Lauren had been drifting in school bored with her classes and her friends and small town life by the coast. The only worry was moving back to East London, so close to where Lauren had lived until she was seven. It didn't matter, Lauren had assured them. They could all do with a change.

Donny came first to London after Christmas and she and Jessica followed a few weeks later. Now it was April and this was the first time she had visited the old house.

She'd thought about it. Her college wasn't far and there'd been some days when she was tempted to go a different route and pass by the end of the street but she never had. They'd been busy settling in, decorating, arranging things where they wanted them. Recently a cat had appeared in the garden and Jessica had tempted it day after day with tit bits and food and now it lived in their house. Jessica had called it Caesar until one day, a couple of weeks before, she'd gone to the cupboard under the stairs and found three kittens in among the old newspapers. Now she called it Cleopatra. Donny had laughed and laughed when Jessica told him.

It was the last time she had heard Donny laughing at anything.

The light went off in the attic of Number 49. Lauren looked at the black window for a few moments. Then she let her eyes drop to the floor below. The room behind the bay window had been her parents' bedroom. A giant room with a huge wardrobe and a chest of drawers which was so solid she could climb up the handles.

Another memory, a picture which wavered into sight. The duvet cover on her parents' bed was satiny and soft and she used to lay the side of her face on it. From where she was she could see the bars of Daisy's cot and Daisy's legs in the air, where she was kicking out. Her mum was moving around in the room, her feet soft on the floor. They were getting ready for bed she thought. All three of them sleeping in the big room.

A window opened and snapped her out of her

9

thoughts. The lights were on and it was like a stage. The lad that she'd seen getting out of the car was standing there. This time he *was* looking at her, staring at her, his eyes like weights on her shoulders. She pulled the collar of her jacket up over the bottom half of her face. She should go. She should just turn and walk away. Her eyes flicked back up to the room though. The lad gave a wave, as if he was on a boat and she was on the dock. But he wasn't, he was standing in her parents' old bedroom.

It was a room she knew well.

Ten years ago she had died and come back to life in that room.

# 2

Jessica was still up when she got back.

'Where have you been?' she demanded.

Lauren was tired. It was almost midnight and she'd walked from Hazelwood Road back to the house. It had taken her over half an hour. The rain had got heavier and she'd had to avoid several loud groups of young lads and a few drunks. Her hair was soaked through. She could feel it lying damply across her shoulders.

She peeled her jacket off without replying. There was no point in talking to Jessica when she was so *angry* all the time. She went straight into the tiny kitchen and took out a bottle of water from the fridge. She could feel Jessica behind her, her eyes boring into her back. In the corner, by the back door, was the cardboard box that held the kittens. Cleopatra was lying on her side. The kittens were feeding from her. Lauren looked at them and felt a stirring inside her. Just a cat that had wandered into the house and attached itself to them. At the beginning it had brought them dead mice, small grey creatures that lay lifeless on the patio. Now it had brought them something better. Kittens, all female. Jessica had given them regal names; Victoria, Alexandra and Juliana.

'Have you been to see Donny?' Jessica said, her voice lower.

''Course not!' Lauren said, pulling her eyes away from the kittens and turning round. 'I just went for a walk. I walked . . .'

She was about to say that she'd walked to the old house but stopped. Jessica was inches from her. Her mouth was twisted to one side and her eyes were darting about. She was standing in one place and yet was in constant movement, her hands clasped, then apart, then rubbing her shoulders and her neck.

'Oh, Jess, come here,' she said, and put her arms out to pull her aunt into her chest.

Jessica seemed to swoon, her head on Lauren's wet hair. Lauren could feel her hot body; agitated, a mass of tics and sharp edges. What had happened to change her lovely cuddly aunt into this wreckage?

Donny had left.

Lauren patted Jessica's back. She was taller and bigger than her aunt and she drew her out of the kitchen and into the living room pulling her towards the settee where they both sat down. She waited for the crying to stop.

'How can he do this to us?' Jessica said, wiping her nose on the sleeve of her T-shirt.

'I don't know.'

'We've been together for eleven years. How can he meet someone else? How can he?'

'He didn't plan for it, Jess, you know that.'

'Why did he make us come all the way from St Agnes

if he was just going to go off with someone else? Why not leave us where we were?'

'It hadn't started then,' Lauren said, her voice slow and steady.

'He says he loves her!'

'Give him time. He *thinks* he loves her. He'll get fed up with her. He'll come back.'

'You think he will?'

''Course he will. He's loved you for eleven years. This has only been a couple of months. He's infatuated.'

'He says she makes him feel young again! I don't get it. I didn't try to make feel *old*.'

'He's thirty-five. It's a life crisis.'

'All that time when we were packing up the house in St Agnes.'

'It wasn't happening then.'

'Why did he have to go to that school? Why did he have to meet her?'

'Give him time to get fed up with her. He'll come back.'

'You're always sticking up for him.'

'I'm not. I just think we should keep calm.'

'It's always been the same. You and Donny ganging up against me. He's not even related to you! He's not even your blood!'

Lauren stiffened. Jessica turned to her, a shocked look on her face, her hand over her mouth.

'Oh my god! What a cow I am. How could I say such a vile thing? No wonder he hates me. You'll be hating me next.'

Lauren sighed and pulled Jessica close.

'Stop it, stop it now. No one hates you. We'll get through this. If you can keep your nerve, give Donny some space then in weeks or a month – he'll get tired of her and come back.'

There was quiet for a minute and Lauren felt Jessica's shoulders easing, her body relaxing.

'You think?'

Lauren nodded. Donny would come back to them. Wouldn't he?

Once Jessica was in bed and Lauren was sure she was asleep she went into the spare room, Donny's study, now a kind of transit area. On the floor was a suitcase and two bags packed. Donny's things, waiting to be picked up and moved to the flat where he was staying with the new woman. Lauren sat down beside them. She pulled the zip of one of the bags open. Jumpers and shoes, higgledy piggledy, put there in a rush.

How unlike Donny. He was so tidy and organised. In St Agnes, where most of his stuff still was, his books and CDs were in alphabetical order, his clothes ironed and hung up, his music magazines stacked in date order. Living with two untidy women had driven him mad. *The toothpaste goes here!* he'd say, pointing at a shelf in the bathroom cupboard. *The towels dry over the rail not over the side of the bath!* Lauren and Jessica had laughed at him.

Was the new woman tidy?

Lauren did the zip of the bag up again. She felt a mild panic in her chest and put her hand over her mouth as if to hold it down. Donny was really leaving. He was taking his stuff and moving it to someone else's shelves and cupboards. Now he would stack his toothbrush in another cupboard in a different bathroom.

*I couldn't help myself,* he'd said.

She remembered the night, a week before, when he tried to explain it to them. Something outside his control had happened to him. He'd been in London on his own for a few weeks. He missed Jessie and Lauren. He'd spent some time with people in his department and had become close to one of the women. They were still in St Agnes, sorting the house out. Nothing happened then. It started weeks later, after Jessie and Lauren got to London. He never thought it would last. It hit him like a thunderbolt, he'd said dramatically and Jessie had swore at him, run at him, clawed at him. He took it all and when she calmed down he kept talking, using his soft, sad voice. *We'll still be in touch,* he'd said, *you're still a big part of my life, both of you.* Jessica had stormed off into her room and banged the door so hard the floorboards trembled. He hadn't gone after her. He turned to Lauren and held her by the shoulders. *Lolly, whatever happens between me and Jessie you'll always be my girl. Always.* Lauren had stiffened but Donny pulled her towards him into a clinch. He held her so tight she could hardly breathe. When he let go of her his face was reddening. She turned away. She didn't want to look at him any more. He said his new flat was nearby. *Only a ten minute walk!* But it might as well have been in Australia.

Donald Greene had been a fixture of Lauren's life ever since the day Jessica brought him to the house in Hazelwood Road. Her mum liked him but she pretended otherwise. *Doesn't that lad have a home of his own?* she'd say when Donny appeared shuffling behind Jessica. He had long hair then and wore baggy jeans and a leather jacket and was always rolling a cigarette. Lauren was fascinated by the process. When her mother was out and Jessica was looking after her she would sit and watch Donny create his roll-ups. Her eyes focused on the small tin he took out and placed on his knees, the tiny white paper that sat quivering on the upended lid as he pinched a finger and thumb full of tobacco. Then came moments of careful pulling and teasing, elongating the brown mass so that it fitted the paper and lay along it. With great care Donny would pick up the fragile concoction and lick along one side of it, turning it with his fingers so it became a cigarette. Then he would start again.

When Lauren's family shattered it was Donny and Jessica who gave her a home, Donny who spent night after night sitting in the armchair by her bed just in case she woke up, in case she was fretting. Donny who took her with him to see the house in St Agnes while Jessica looked after the sale of her mum's house and furniture. Donny, who cut his hair and bought a suit and got a job as a Maths teacher. The roll-ups disappeared and were replaced by slim packets with health warnings. Eventually he gave them up. *You can't smoke with a child around the house,* Jessica had said. He had been a second dad to her and now he was leaving.

Lauren got up from where she'd been sitting on the floor. She gave the bags a half-hearted kick. She'd already lost one family and now it looked as though she was losing another.

# 3

Lauren went back to Hazelwood Road. It was two weeks since she'd gone to see her childhood home and she felt a need to have another look, in the daylight. When college was over she made her way out of the building and had to shrug off Julie Bell.

'I'm not going your way. I'm meeting someone,' she said, as Julie got into step with her.

'Who?' Julie asked. 'A lad?'

'No!' Lauren said, shaking her head.

Julie was always thinking about the opposite sex. During the very first conversation they had at the end of an Art class she had asked, *Did you leave a boyfriend behind in Cornwall?* Lauren shook her head smiling at this girl's directness. *I'm in love with this lad,* Julie had said, *but I haven't got the courage to tell him.*

Lauren hadn't left anyone behind. She'd changed the subject asking Julie where she'd bought the dress she was wearing. It was quite unlike anything she had seen on anyone else. *It's vintage. I got it from a charity shop,* Julie had said, looking pleased at the compliment. Then she'd looked at Lauren's hair and said, *Wow, your hair is long. Can I style it for you?*

That day, outside the college, Julie seemed to lose interest in where Lauren was going and her gaze drifted towards a tall black boy in a football shirt who had just come out of the main doors. Ryan Lassiter; the love of her life.

'See you, then . . .' Lauren said.

Julie gave a distracted nod, her eyes clinging to the boy as he threaded his way through the throng of students.

Lauren turned away and headed in the direction of Hazelwood Road. She walked along the High Street, the noise of traffic in her ears. She lowered her head and cut across the stationary cars, vans and lorries. Every now and again there was a bus hissing and gasping and edging forward a few metres forward before stopping again. There were faces staring out of the windows; a couple of grey-haired women, one behind the other; some teenagers in school uniform, a bald man, his scalp smooth and shiny. Faces that were closed up, trance-like.

Everywhere in London was so crowded, so crammed with people and cars. Stepping back onto the pavement she had to pause to let some mums go by with their pushchairs. She gathered her hair up and pulled it back off her face. With one hand she held it at the base of her neck. With the other she got out a hairband and fastened it. She felt cooler immediately. A siren started, a whooping sound which seemed to be coming from a nearby car alarm. It cut across the sound of thudding music from a high up window. She put her hands over her ears and walked on, her head down, blocking out the people and cars, the sights and sounds. She imagined she had heavy earphones on muffling the noise as if she was underwater.

In St Agnes, in the summer, she often swam out into the sea, stopped and trod water looking back at the shore. The pebbly beach was dotted with people who were dwarfed by the cliffs and the vast sky. It never occurred to her that the beach was empty. It was just normal. Sometimes she stopped moving her legs and let herself sink down into the sea, the water closing over her head. She didn't open her eyes, just hung for a few seconds in silence that was as thick as cotton wool. Surfacing she shook the water from her ears and heard the gulls above and maybe the sound of boat or a single car or a tinny radio from somewhere. There, by the sea, she actively looked and listened for new things. In London she was ambushed by raucous noise and constantly changing scenery; people, buildings, cars and rubbish.

Had she noticed these things when she was a young child, living day in day out in this city? Probably not. It was just normal. In any case her world had been *inside* her house, her room, her toys, her dressing-up box, her mother's doll's house, her books and paints and cassettes. Whenever she went out it was always with her mum, in the car or walking beside the pushchair. Her mum would never have allowed her to play out on the street; she knew that, Jessica had told her. *Grace hardly ever let you out of her sight.* Then, at seven, she had been plucked out of London and taken to Cornwall. Now, ten years later, she had been dropped back in.

She turned into Hazelwood Road. How different it was to that night when it had been dark and raining. Then it had been gloomy and quiet. At four-fifteen in the afternoon it was alive with movement and noise and colour. Groups of school kids lingered along the pavement. She went forward slowly, passing them, looking round at each step. She passed a doctor's surgery and a small block of flats with balconies that hung over the street. On the other side of the road was a bus stop where a line of teenage boys were waiting behind an old man and a dog. Up ahead was a long line of terraced houses. Her old house was fifty metres or so away. This time she stayed on the same side of the road and walked, her head down slightly, until she came to it.

She turned to look. In the daylight it looked shabby. She glanced along the terrace. The other houses were in good condition but this house – her house – was run down, uncared for. The window frames were peeling and the window sills, at least on the ground floor, were crumbling. The side window in the front bay was cracked and someone had put masking tape across it. The front door was solid wood with no glass at all. It was green; she could see some of the brush strokes where it had been painted in a hurry. The number, 49, had been put on in cheap plastic lettering, the 9 slightly lower than the other number. At the side of the door were three bells. They must have been put there when the house had been divided into flats and rented out. Now it was to be restored by a single family. Lauren thought she'd seen one of them a couple of weeks before, getting out of a taxi, returning home after a trip.

She focused on the space that had once been a front garden. The wall along the edge had been knocked down and the ground sloped towards the road. It was a place to park cars even though there were none there at that moment. There was rubbish; piles of fittings that had been taken out of the house, planks of wood, cupboards, empty cardboard boxes. In the far corner was a bathtub and two shower trays, piled up. By the side of the front door was a green wheelie bin. She'd noticed none of this the first time she came. The messy contents of the front of the house had been hidden by the dark.

There was a sudden movement under the bathtub. A large ginger cat slid out, its body long and thin. When it was standing it seemed to spring back into shape, its fur bristling. It lifted a paw and licked it ignoring her. She thought of Cleopatra back at the house. Just that morning Jessica had found the cardboard box in the kitchen empty. It had sent her into a momentary panic. After a few moments of searching, Cleopatra and the kittens were found in the space between the sofa and the curtains. She had moved the kittens in the night. *It's her way of protecting them from predators*, Jessica had said, relief written over her face.

The ginger cat in front of Lauren leapt gracefully onto the wheelie bin. It turned its back to her and she immediately felt silly. She swivelled away and looked down the street. What was she doing there? She was too close, too near; she needed some distance between herself and this house. She strode on, ten paces, twenty. She crossed the street and walked back up the other side. Standing at an angle she looked again past the front garden at the building itself. Now it just looked like any other property, bricks and mortar; a semi detached, three-storey dwelling.

She rested her eye on the side entrance, a wooden gate which led through to the back garden. When she lived there it had been the gate through which her mother pulled the dustbin. Had it been a wheelie bin then? She couldn't remember. She tried because it seemed important that these memories came back. She focused on the green bin but something else pushed itself into her head. An image that only stayed for a second. A face. A painted face. Not a picture but a face with thick paint on it, so thick you could almost see the brush strokes.

A clown.

The door to Number 53 opened and a woman came out. Lauren instantly recognised her. Molly. One of their neighbours. She took a step onto the road, waited for a car to go past and then crossed. Molly who had had long ginger hair and who wore lace up black boots most of the time. She had twin girls who were a couple of years older than Lauren. The girls were identical she remembered and were always whispering to each other.

Molly was picking up what looked like junk mail from

her doormat and then came out of the house with a handful of leaflets. She left the door open, walked to the bin and put the leaflets in. Her hair wasn't as ginger as Lauren remembered but it was hanging in curls. There were no black boots either just sandals. Other than that she was the same. As if ten years hadn't passed. As if Lauren had gone to the shops with her mum and was returning home an hour later. Without thinking about it she walked towards the low garden wall and called out.

'Molly!'

Molly looked up, her eye settling on Lauren, a half-smile ready on her lips. She frowned instead and looked to the side as if the call had come from somewhere else.

'Molly, it's Lauren,' she said, walking up to the garden wall.

'Sorry, Lauren? I don't know . . .'

'I used to live a couple of houses away?'

Molly's face was pinched into puzzlement. She didn't recognise her. Of course not. She'd changed. Her hair was longer. She was all grown up. A second later Molly smiled.

'I don't believe it! Little Lauren?'

Lauren nodded.

'My god! How are you? I heard you were living in Devon.'

'Cornwall.'

'Right . . .'

There was a moment's unease. Molly seemed on the

brink of saying things and then didn't. Lauren filled the silence.

'I'm up in London for a while. I'm at the college, at Bethnal Green?'

Molly nodded.

'I couldn't resist coming . . . Just to see,' she gestured towards Number 49, two houses along.

Molly looked to the side her eyes resting on the house then moving slowly back to Lauren.

'Oh, Lauren, I never saw you afterwards, after that day. And you were just a little girl! I wanted to say something to you but how could I? Your aunty took you out of hospital. Then I heard you'd moved.'

'I did! We lived at the seaside,' Lauren said, her words racing, pulling away from dangerous ground. 'How are the twins?'

'They're great. At university! They've just finished their second year and they're going off travelling. I hardly see them now.'

Lauren gave a polite nod. She had never been friends with the twins.

'I miss them, I do. And you? How are you?'

'I'm fine.'

From the house came the sound of ringing.

'My phone,' Molly said.

Lauren nodded and took a step to the side, as if she was keen to get off. 'I must go. Give my regards to the twins.'

Molly walked backwards nodding her head. She seemed about to go inside but changed direction coming forward again, close up to Lauren, putting a hand on her arm, leaving hardly any space between them.

'I went to your father's trial,' she said, in a low voice. 'I was there on that last day, when the verdict came in. When they said *Guilty* there was a cheer. Everyone in the public gallery stood up and cheered. Justice was done, Lauren. At least you can be thankful for that.'

Molly went back into the house, giving a little wave before she pulled the front door closed. Lauren turned as if to go but found herself looking down at the pavement, her chest swirling with emotion. In her ears she could hear a cheering sound, like a crowd at a football match. *Her father's trial.* She hadn't heard those words said aloud for many years. She walked blindly, head down, putting one foot in front of the other. A strand of hair fell across her face and she hooked it back around her ear. After ten or twelve steps she collided with someone.

'Watch where you're going!'

She lifted her head but not before she noticed that a plastic carrier bag had split and its contents were on the pavement. She glanced up at the face of a lad and then looked down at the ground where some potatoes and onions had spilled, a couple rolling near the kerb. She said *sorry* a couple of times and squatted down to pick up the vegetables. The lad had placed his other bag on the ground and was scooping up a couple of onions.

'The bag's no good,' she said, seeing the split across the bottom. Both her hands held potatoes and onions. She stood up. When she looked again at the lad she recognised him. It was the boy that she had seen going into her old house. Then he had been up at the first floor window. Now he was standing with a Tesco carrier bag in one hand and potatoes in the other. His curly hair looked untidy, as if it hadn't been combed. He had stubble on his face.

'Do I know you?' he said, smiling at her.

She shook her head, offering the vegetables to him. He adopted a hopeless stance. He had nowhere to put them.

'I only live here,' he said, gesturing to her old house. 'You can put those in my pocket. Look, I'm sure I know you.'

'Are you sure you want me to . . .'

She held the vegetables up as he nodded and then leaned across him to put some in one pocket and some in the other. His jacket was undone. Underneath he had a T-shirt with the word *Cuba* on it. Close up she avoided making eye contact. She could smell the faint scent of deodorant. The other carrier bag was too heavy, she could see that. In a few moments its handle would break.

'You'd better go,' she said.

'I do know you from somewhere,' he said.

She shook her head, sidestepped him and walked on, leaving him with his fragile shopping bag and pockets full of root vegetables. She kept her eyes firmly in front and walked past the flats and the doctor's surgery. A bus was just leaving the stop. The schoolboys had gone but the man with the dog was still there. She went on towards the high road and her bus stop. She would not go there again.

Hanging around the street, walking backwards and forwards past the house like a lost puppy. She rubbed her hands together. They felt gritty from vegetables.

She would leave Number 49 behind her.

It was someone else's house now.

# 4

Jessica wasn't in when Lauren got home but Donny was there, sitting at the kitchen table, reading through his post. Beside him was a small pile of opened envelopes and discarded letters or bills. He must have used his own key to let himself in.

'Hi,' she said, hooking her bag over the back of a kitchen chair.

'Good day?' he said, giving her a tentative smile.

She shrugged.

'Mine's been hell. Some Year Ten brings a knife into class and threatens someone. On top of that there's a bad inspection report about the department and I've got to read it before an eight-fifteen meeting tomorrow morning. It's been one of those days.'

She made an *um* sound and Donny went back to looking at his papers. Swapping chit-chat with him as though he hadn't moved out wasn't something she wanted to do. Although there was a lot she could have told him. Her Drama class was putting short plays together which would be shown to the other groups the following week. Her History essay had been given a B plus and she'd decided on the subject of her Art study, doll's houses or, as the books called them, *Dollhouses*. She could have told Donny these things but she didn't want to.

What she would have really liked to do was to tell him about the trip to Hazelwood Road and how she'd met her old neighbour. In the past, when she'd had things to say about her family, it was usually Donny who she talked to. Jessica was different. With Jessica, mentioning her young life, when she lived with her mum and Daisy, was like touching a raw wound. She avoided it.

Looking at Donny, flicking through his letters and bills, she wanted to put a hand out and touch him and ask him if he'd been there on that day of her father's trial. *What happened when the foreman of the jury read out the verdict? Was there a cheer from everyone?* That's what she wanted to ask. But Donny's face was concentrating on a flier from an insurance company so she pulled out a chair and sat down feeling awkward, as if it was she who didn't live in the flat any more, not Donny.

'Drink?' he said, not looking at her.

She shook her head. He stood up and took a glass from the drainer then turned to the fridge. The naturalness with which he did it made her instantly annoyed. She watched as he pulled the door open and took out a bottle of water, shuffling around in the freezer for some ice cubes. When he sat down again she had to say something.

'You shouldn't be acting as though you still live here.'

He sighed.

'Where's Jessie?' he said.

'Why do you want to know?' she said.

'She said she'd be here. That's all,' he said, rotating his glass so that the ice clinked against the sides.

'She's working.'

Donny looked up. 'She's got a job?'

'Just temping. A couple of weeks in an office.'

'That's good. It's good that she's doing something. Getting on with stuff. Look, Lolly, it's the best thing. For her to move on.'

She wished he wouldn't call her *Lolly* but she didn't want to say it. It was Jessica who had started the name, much to the annoyance of her mum. Had her father ever called her Lolly? She couldn't remember. Jessica had stopped years before. Now Donny was the only person who used it. It was a sign of affection, she knew but she didn't feel so close to him at the moment.

She watched as he drank his water and pulled a letter out of an envelope. It had been ripped across so he'd already looked at it. Most likely he didn't know what to say either. She noticed his shirt then, and the darkness of his jacket next to it. He looked different, sharper somehow, his shoulders a straight line, his collar stiff, his tie knotted as if by machine, perfect, neat, smart. Even his hair was shorter, standing up at the front, shiny with gel.

'Is that a new suit?' she said.

He waved his hand in a dismissive gesture.

'I bought it ages ago. After I got the job.'

'I've never seen it before,' Lauren said.

Why was he lying? Lauren knew what Donny owned. They'd lived together for ten years. She knew the contents of all his drawers and his wardrobe. She knew what was inside his rucksack and his pockets. She knew Donny inside out. When he asked where something was Lauren could jump up and get it in a second. *Where's my reading glasses? Where's my book? My iPod? Where on earth are my shin-pads?* Lauren knew Donny. She had mapped him out, she knew every place. Donny was familiar territory. She just *knew* him.

On the kitchen chair, next to where he was sitting, was a briefcase. It was dark brown leather, hard and rounded at the top. It didn't fit the chair, its ends jutting over the edges. She must have been staring at it because Donny spoke.

'That *is* new. A birthday present . . .'

He didn't finish his sentence. No doubt he was going to say that it was from his girlfriend, Alison.

'You said you'd never carry a briefcase. You said they're stuffy and pompous.'

'It's handy, it holds everything and it looks smart.'

'Did *she* buy it for you?'

He shrugged his shoulders.

'Look at you. Wearing a new suit, carrying a briefcase. You're like a different person. You've even had your hair cut differently!' Lauren said, her voice trembling.

'The suit is not new, Lolly. I've had it since Easter. Maybe you didn't notice it before . . .'

The front door sounded and Lauren heard Jessica's voice calling out. Lauren stared at Donny, trying to see his reaction at Jessica's arrival, looking for signs of sadness or regret. For the second time she wanted to reach out and touch his hand and say, *It's Jessie, your Jessie.* He'd sat back in the chair though and was gathering his post up from the table squaring the edges and holding it in front of him like a screen.

'I'm back,' Jessica said throwing the kitchen door open, her hands holding carrier bags, 'Donny! I didn't see your car.'

Jessica dumped the bags on the work surface and turned back, her face bright, her manner polite. It was false, Lauren knew, like a mask.

'How are you?' she said, cheerfully.

'Good. Good. I thought you'd be here so I got dropped off in the car. When you weren't here I let myself in. I hope that's OK.'

''Course it is. It's your . . . I still think of this as *your* home.'

Donny's eyes dropped to the table and he shifted about uneasily. Cleopatra appeared suddenly and walked through Jessica's legs, turning a circle and then doing it again, her tail high up in the air.

''Course, most of this is junk mail. I don't know why I bothered,' he said.

'Don't feel you have make excuses to come here. You can come here any time. Just drop by. Make yourself at home.'

Donny stood up and brushed down his clothes. When Lauren had been rude to him he'd seemed relaxed. Now that Jessica was being nice he was distinctly uneasy.

He reached over for his briefcase but before he could get to it Jessica slipped in between his arms and put her hands around his neck and buried her face in his chest. Donny's eyes closed. Whether it was with irritation or pleasure Lauren couldn't tell. Lauren turned away and stole out of the room. She let the kitchen door shut and went upstairs and sat down on the landing. The house was so small that she could still hear the mumble of their voices. She strained to listen closer hoping that Jessica wasn't crying. She heard them talking, quietly. Jessica saying something, then Donny, then Jessica replying. It was all on an even keel. Maybe the things she had said to Jessica were true. Give Donny time and he would come back. Make him feel at home, make him see that this was where he belonged and one day he would walk back through that front door and stay.

There were sounds of movement and the kitchen door opened. Donny came out first. Lauren could see his shoulders. He was carrying his briefcase and using his other hand to comb through his hair. At the front door he stopped patting his pocket. He turned back to Jessica. Lauren slid back onto the landing out of sight.

'This came to my school. It's for Lolly.'

There was quiet. Lauren couldn't hear any reply from Jessica. The silence was heavy with looks and body language that she couldn't see.

'You should give it to her.'

'Why was it sent there? How does *he* know you've moved schools? How can *he* know that?' Jessica said.

'Look at the address. It was sent to my old school in St Agnes. They forwarded it on. You know he's written to me before, years ago.'

'You threw away the letters though,' Jessica said, her voice dropping to a loud whisper.

'I did. 'Course I did. But this one's not addressed to me. It's for Lolly and I think she should open it.'

'I don't know,'

'She's seventeen, Jessie. She has to know that he's been writing to her. You can't keep it from her forever.'

'I'll think about it.'

'I have to go.'

There was quiet again and Lauren edged closer to the top of the stairs. She could see Jessica's back and Donny's suit. They were close together and the silence was palpable.

'I'll give you a call, make sure you're OK.'

Jessica took a step back and the front door opened. In a second it had closed and Donny was gone. She turned and walked back up the hallway. Lauren stood up and came quietly down the stairs. In the kitchen Jessica was standing with her back to the units, her arms behind her.

'It's just good to see him. It's nice to have him back here, at home, even for a little while,' she said, lightly.

Lauren looked at the table and round the work surfaces. She couldn't see the letter.

'Can I see it?' she said.

'What?'

'The letter. It's for me, isn't it? I overheard Donny saying it.'

Jessica seemed to bristle.

'Where is it? Is it behind your back? Come on. You don't want me to guess which hand it's in, do you?'

Jessica let her arms drop. In one hand was the letter crumpled up. She opened her palm and seemed to hesitate.

'Please?'

'There, take it. You must know who it's from.'

Lauren was about to say *No*, but something was unfolding in her head, something that had been packed away long ago. *Guess which hand it's in?* The words were familiar. She took the envelope and saw that the address of Donny's school in St Agnes had been roughly crossed out with a thin black felt and the words *forwarded to* above the new school address. The original writing was slanted and faint as though the writer wasn't sure that they should write it at all. Looking down at it an odd picture came into her head. A face painted the purest white with red lips and a red nose, round like a boiled sweet. A clown's face.

'It's from Slater,' Jessica said.

The face dissolved and she stared at the letter in her hand. Her father, Robert Slater, had written to her from his prison cell.

# 5

Lauren folded the letter in half and took it to her room.

She sat on her bed and kicked her shoes off pulling her legs up underneath her. She smoothed the envelope out on the duvet and looked at it. It's from *Slater*. The sound of her father's name coming from Jessica's mouth had startled her. It was a word that she hardly ever heard spoken out loud since the trial, since going to live in Cornwall. Mostly she had heard it in formal sentences. There were letters from solicitors or communications from the social services and three or four cards from her paternal grandparents who had moved to Northumberland. *Your father, Robbie Slater, is in good health and he misses you as we do, Love Nana Jo and Granddad Ray.*

Robert Slater is being transferred to Strangeways, Manchester.

Robert Slater has lost his appeal against a life sentence.

Mr R Slater has asked us to forward this birthday card to his daughter.

Mr Robert Slater, forty-eight-year-old builder, maintains his innocence and says he will fight to have his name cleared.

These communications were read out grudgingly by

Jessica. Then they were folded up and shoved away somewhere. Lauren knew, at these times, that it wasn't a good idea to prolong the conversation; the mention of her father's name was always a bad thing. A shadow in the corner of the room, a black crow hovering at the edge of their lives.

Today Jessica had just called him *Slater*. It had come out of her mouth easily like chewing gum spat away. *Slater*.

Across from her bed she caught her reflection in the mirror that sat on her desk. Her face looked long and thin, her dark eyes sinking inwards. She stared at herself for a moment. Her brown hair hung loose down each side of her face. She rarely wore it this way. She plaited it, or tied it back. Sometimes she used a variety of soppy Disney clips and slides to hold it off her face, the kind worn by children. She touched one side of it letting her fingers go right to the end. It was bitty and probably should be trimmed. She hadn't had it cut for ten years though.

She opened the envelope and pulled the paper out that was inside. She was surprised to see that it was printed, her father's name at the top, centred, Robert B Slater. It had been done on a computer. Her eye slid down the page to the bottom, to the signature. It was scrawny, not straight, more like a pattern, the R and the S standing tall and the rest dissolving into squiggles.

She tried to focus on the page in front of her but inside her chest was liquid. Her ribs seemed fluid. She closed her eyes for a moment and tried to work out what was going on. Fear? Sadness? Bitterness? Were these emotions swirling round, melding together? Filling her up? She slumped back. She couldn't identify any particular emotion. It was like when she first went to see the house in Hazelwood Road. Then she had tried to summon up her feelings from ten years before. Then, as now, she'd felt empty save for the odd jigsaw piece of memory.

The letter was short. Lauren made herself read it over twice. As she did so she could hear Jessica below banging about in the kitchen. It sounded as though she'd put the radio on. Band music, someone singing, a horn playing and violins. Then suddenly it stopped and there was silence. Then the contents of the letter seemed more solemn.

*Dear Lauren, It's some time since I wrote. I hear, through the family grapevine, that you are well and that makes me feel good. I am reasonably healthy although the docs have put me on tablets for high blood pressure and I have some new inhalers for my asthma.*

*The reason I'm writing after such a long time is to let you know that my second appeal is being heard in the high court this autumn. At present the date is 3rd September but that could change. My solicitor is hopeful. I wanted to let you know about this because of course, like the first appeal, all those years ago, there will be publicity and I know you will be affected by it all.*

*I'm sorry for that. I would never do anything to hurt you. I think of you every day and wonder what you are like. Maybe, when this is all over, you and I might see each other again.*

*You were only a little girl. I never forget that for one moment.*

*One thing I absolutely want you to know. I don't blame you for what has happened to me. Not for one moment. Never.*

*Much, much love, Dad.*

Lauren looked up. She could hear Jessica's steps on the stairs. She half expected a knock on the door and Jessica's face to appear but her aunt walked past and went into her own room. She should really get up and go in there and show Jessica the letter from her father. She needed to know what was happening. He was making a second appeal and there would be publicity. He was worried about the effect it would have on her.

She stared at the paper, at the neatly printed words and the erratic signature at the end. Along the bottom, printed in different font, was the address of the prison. *HMPS Nunchester nr Durham.* It was in the north. Was that why her grandparents had moved to Northumberland? To be near their son? Or just to get as far away as they could from London?

A second appeal.

The first appeal happened when she was nine. She remembered Jessica and Donny telling her about it and explaining that it would last for a day or two and that it might be in the newspapers again. Just in case anyone at school or in the town had said anything. Not that anyone In St Agnes would have linked Lauren Ashe to an appeal in the high court on behalf of Robert Slater, serving a life sentence for a double murder. She had taken her mum's maiden name and no one in St Agnes knew about what had happened to bring them there, this mix and match family; Donny Greene, Jessica and Lauren Ashe, fugitives from East London, from Hazelwood Road.

She folded the letter up. The new appeal would be another court case, she supposed. She'd seen enough of them in television dramas. She'd never been in court herself. At seven she'd been too young to go and stand in a witness box. No, she'd gone to Exeter with Jessica and Donny, to the police station there. It was a modern glass building with people going in and out of rooms and telephones ringing. She remembered that she'd been wearing her new school uniform. She hadn't wanted to wear it but Jessica had insisted. After a summer of lazing around on the beach all her clothes looked washed out, old, faded, slightly too small. They felt gritty when she put them on as though the sand had been ingrained into the fabric. The only smart thing she had was her school uniform, a green gingham dress that hung just below her knees, a blazer, white socks and black shoes.

They took her up in a lift to the top of the building. When the doors opened they were faced with a carpeted waiting area and soft chairs like someone's front room. There were pictures on the wall, and a table with a kettle and mugs on it, a small wicker basket full of tea bags and sachets of instant coffee, drinking chocolate, sugar and powered milk. In the corner was a play area; huge red bean bags and a rocking toy, some trains, some building bricks, a white board with felts. It also had a low table on top of which was a squiggly strip of metal shaped like a continuous W. Threaded along it were different shaped coloured beads which had to be moved from one end to the other. She couldn't take her eyes off it. Her fingers twitched to play with it.

A woman came out of a room. She said she was a policewoman but Lauren couldn't really believe it. She was wearing jeans and a light pink sweatshirt with a fairy pattern on it. She had long earrings on. Each one was a chain on which hung a silver butterfly. They swung when she shook her head or nodded. How could this woman be a policewoman dressed like that?

They would go in soon the woman said and Jessica and Donny would be able to stay in the room with her. Only Lauren would have to sit in the chair opposite the camera. It was important, the policewoman said, that neither Donny nor Jessica spoke to Lauren or made any communication with her like mouthing words or nodding or shaking their heads.

When the woman left they sat for a while. Lauren was in between Jessica and Donny and each of them was holding one of her hands. They were quiet although after a few moments Jessica whispered, *Just tell the truth. That's all you can do.* Of course she would tell the truth. That's all she knew. After a while she looked longingly over at the table with the wire and the beads on it. Would it be OK to ask if she could play with it? Would *playing* be an OK thing to do at this serious time? She sensed not so she sat rigidly until a door opened further up the corridor and the same woman emerged gesturing for them to approach. As they got nearer to her she saw the woman smile brightly and the butterflies swayed, fluttering about the woman's chin.

Inside there was a large comfortable chair. Over one arm of it was a pink furry snake, its head resting on the carpet. She sat down and pulled it up until its flat face was looking at her, its sting protruding from its mouth, a piece of black felt.

Bright lights went on.

*We need these for the camera*, the woman with the earrings said.

On one side was Jessica, a shaky smile on her face. On the other was Donny, straightening his collar, twisting his neck from side to side as if his shirt was too tight for him.

*We're just about ready to start now*, the woman said, *you need to look at the screen and answer the barrister's questions as honestly as you can. Are you ready Lauren? Do you understand what is happening here? If you feel you want to stop you just have to say – I want to stop – and we will take a break.*

*I'm ready*, Lauren said, twisting the pink snake round and round her arm. I'm ready.

Are you ready?

I'm ready.

There was a knock on Lauren's bedroom door. It broke her thoughts and she looked towards it. She expected it to open but it stayed shut. Usually Jessica knocked on her door and came straight in.

'Come in, Jess,' she called.

The door opened and Jessica looked apologetic as if

she'd done something wrong. She glanced down at the letter on the duvet.

'You all right?' she said.

She was holding something. A pink plastic file with a popper fastening. Lauren nodded, shrugged her shoulders. What was there to say? Her father had written to her.

'Thing is,' Jessica said, 'That's not the only letter you got. Slater's been writing to you ever since he went to prison. I never showed them to you.'

Lauren looked at the pink file again. It was stretched at the bottom, full up with envelopes.

'Donny and I made the decision that at seven years old you were too young to read these things. In the first couple of years he wrote a lot but then it got less. I guess the fact that no one answered him put him off. I even sent some of them back and he started sending them to Donny's school. He got the message though. After three or four years it was down to two a year and then just one. On your birthday. Until that new letter.'

Jessica held out the file and Lauren took it. The plastic was hard, its edges sharp. She frowned. She had already read one letter from her father. Was it necessary for her to read more?

'For years now Donny's been saying that I should give you these but it never seemed the right time. I guess, now, what with everything being up and down . . . Anyway, he's right. You're seventeen. You should have them now.'

Lauren placed the folder on the bed and held the opened letter up.

'My father says there's going to be another appeal,' she said.

Jessica shook her head.

'He does,' Lauren said, thinking that Jessica disbelieved her.

'No,' Jessica said, her hand up in front of her, 'I'm not disagreeing. It's just I can't . . . I don't want to talk about him. I just can't.'

'It's OK,' Lauren said, softly, feeling uncomfortable.

Jessica stood up as if to go but paused and then sat down again.

'I can't even think about that man without feeling a sort of nausea inside. I know he's your father but he took my sister and my niece away.'

'I know,' Lauren said, feeling her throat thickening.

'Your mum was not an easy person. She was difficult, anxious, a bit bossy. But she was everything to me; sister, mother, friend.'

'I know how close you were.'

Jessica blinked and rubbed her eyes. When she opened them they were glassy with tears.

'Here I am, ten years later, still weeping about it.'

'I do as well,' Lauren said.

''Course you do. She was your lovely mummy. And poor Daisy, not even a year old . . .'

Lauren nodded her head. She felt too emotional to speak.

'In those last months I knew that things weren't right for her. Slater had left her, he came back, then left again. It was like a sort of torture. She never knew where she was with him. I told her to get someone else. She was a nice looking woman, a bit thin but pretty and when she was in a good mood she could be funny and good company. All she needed was someone to love her and all she got was Slater. I'm sorry. I know he's your father but I can't even think about him without wanting smash a plate against the wall. If he's having another appeal then I don't want to know about it. As far as I'm concerned he's dead and buried.'

Jessica stopped and was looking round the room distractedly. Lauren stroked her arm. Her aunt's forehead was in lines, her mouth bunched up to one side.

'I shouldn't have gone to Spain,' she said, 'I shouldn't have left her on her own.'

From outside the room there was sound, a cry, then another. It was Cleopatra meowing for her food. Lauren pictured the kittens downstairs stumbling round behind the sofa wondering where their mother had gone. Jessica got up, opened the door and looked out.

'There'll probably be publicity,' Lauren said.

'I'll avoid it. If you're sensible you'll do the same.'

The meowing was continuing and Jessica was looking flustered.

'I ought to feed this animal,' she said.

Lauren nodded and then her aunt was gone, padding down the stairs using a funny high voice to talk to

Cleopatra. She turned the pink folder over and pulled at the popper. Picking the new letter up she took one last look before putting it in its envelope. Her eyes rested on the last line.

*I don't blame you for what has happened to me. Not for one moment. Never.*

The words stirred up some anger. All the vague feelings in her chest seemed to harden. He didn't *blame* her. What for? Why should she be blamed? She had only told the truth. She had said what she saw, said what had happened. If it hadn't been for her there would have been no eye witness, no one left to tell. She shoved the letter into the pink folder and snapped it shut, putting force on the popper until she heard it click.

She had survived. How could she be blamed for anything?

# 6

The Museum of Childhood was just a walk away from college. Lauren thought it would be a good place to get more inspiration for the theme *The Child in Play*. It was lunchtime and Julie tagged along.

'We can get some food in the café there. It's really good,' Julie said.

The building was huge and as they went into the entrance hall Lauren's eye was drawn to a giant doll's house in a glass case. She walked across to it. A sign underneath said *Amy Miles' House 1890*. It was on three floors and had stairs up the middle to each floor and rooms leading off each side. Her eye was drawn to the bathroom with its white bath and copper water heaters. Underneath was a billiard's room and on the other side of the house a children's play room. A miniature boy stood next to a tiny rocking horse. Next to them was a desk with a reading stand on it and a book was open with microscopic print. She angled her head to see if she could read any of the words. She couldn't.

'Come on,' Julie said, 'there's a whole section on dolls' houses inside.'

It was a big hall, the size of a football pitch and the

ceiling was high, two or three storeys. There was a balcony around the edge of the space and they went up onto it and found the rest of the doll's houses, ten or so dating from different periods of history. Some of them were just as big as the one in the entrance hall. They all opened at the front showing the workings of the house inside. The furniture and decorations and figures all represented the period in which the house was built.

Lauren could have looked at them for hours but she felt Julie's impatience.

'I'm starving!'

They walked down towards the café and while Julie was queuing up to get the food Lauren got a table and thought about her mum's doll's house. It was an antique and couldn't be played with very often. It opened and closed at the front and looked like a model of an old fashioned house with windows and a front door. Looking through the windows she could see the furniture and figures, the wallpaper and rugs, the fireplaces and ornaments and wall hangings. The only way to play with it was to pull a catch at the side so that the front panel opened up. Then she could move the figures from room to room, tidy up the dishes and rearrange the chairs or the sofa or move the piano to a new place.

This was only allowed on special occasions. The doll's house had been given to Lauren's mum by her own mother and was to be shared between her and her sister, Jessica. Whenever she did allow her to play with it she was always telling her to be careful. She said that one day, when Jessica was married and had a family of her own, she would get the doll's house. It was only fair. Her mother had had it for all these years, soon it would be Jessica's turn.

Now it sat in the loft of their house in St Agnes.

Julie came back with two baked potatoes and coleslaw and some drinks. They talked for a few moments about the preparation for the Art exam. Lauren had definitely decided to do something on doll's houses. The question was, how could she make it interesting and *mean* something, *say* something about childhood? Julie had decided to look at building bricks, Lego and the like and work on something three dimensional. She didn't know what yet. They'd been talking about it for a few minutes when Julie suddenly changed the subject.

'Do you think Ryan's good looking?'

Lauren sighed and tried to picture Ryan Lassiter.

'How good looking? Marks out of ten,' Julie said.

'I can't.'

'Go on, marks out of ten.'

She thought hard. His face was in her head but mostly, when she thought of Ryan, she thought of his stiff jeans and smooth polo shirt.

'Six out of ten?' she said.

'Oh no. I'd have said eight.'

Julie went on talking about Ryan and what she liked about him. Lauren didn't mind. It was easy talk, funny and silly and often rude. It had no real substance, no deep meanings, no underlying messages. Unlike her talks at home with Jessica which were becoming increasingly frustrating. Jessica wanted to pour over the details of hers and Donny's relationship and their break-up. She needed constant reassurance. When she wasn't talking about that she was moaning about her temp job or the house or saying that she wished she was back in St Agnes. Once or twice she'd referred to Lauren's father's letters. This was something that Lauren didn't let her go on about. She simply said she hadn't read them and didn't intend to. That, at least, seemed to quell Jessica's irritation. That one thing, among everything else, brought a tiny smile of satisfaction to her aunt's face.

Being with Julie Bell was like a holiday; like eating ice cream and ring doughnuts, being back at the seaside on a breezy hot day, the sand caked between her toes.

'And Ryan's really bright? In Law he's always first to answer the questions. Always has a good point to make.' Julie said, wistfully.

Lauren took a forkful of potato and salad from her plate. She found herself looking at what Julie was wearing. Today it was a short pink shirt dress over some white leggings. Her hair, which was cut asymmetrically, curled round her jaw on one side and was short, to her ear, on the other. Around it was a thick deep pink band, like a scarf, which hung down one side. Lauren wasn't sure which particular vintage look Julie was going for. Sixties? Forties? Maybe it was a mesh. She didn't look bad, not at all. Some days she looked beautiful. Other days she looked startling, alarming even.

'Do you think he's good in bed?' Julie said.

Lauren took a last mouthful of potato and pushed her dish away. She pictured Ryan Lassiter as she'd last seen him. Standing outside the college library that morning. He had a West Ham football shirt on. Lauren was willing to bet that he had designer jeans and expensive trainers on. Ryan was like many of the college lads, wearing the same makes, always well tailored, their stuff pressed and clean, their trainers box-fresh. He was a pleasant enough clone. She wondered about him *in bed*. She moved back from the table as a lad in a starched white apron picked their dishes up, wiping the surface over with a cloth.

'How'd you mean in bed?' she asked, feigning innocence. '*Sleeping*, you mean?'

'You know,' Julie laughed, '*rocking and rolling*.'

Lauren tried to imagine Ryan ripping his clothes off with passion. The picture wouldn't come. He would probably spend a lot of the time folding his stuff up and putting it in a neat pile. Meanwhile Julie would have flung off her evening dress and stiletto heels and would be lying under the covers, only her mad hair and her rosebud red lips on show.

'Marks out of ten?'

'I don't know!'

Lauren didn't know. She'd had one boyfriend in St Agnes but it had all been pretty tame stuff. They'd kissed and cuddled but as soon as he'd become more demanding she'd stopped liking him. In any case she wasn't the sort of girl that boys went for. She didn't wear fashionable clothes or make-up. She didn't enjoy all the strutting and swearing of the boys. She preferred to spend time with Jessica and Donny. When she was younger she'd liked going out with her friends, down to the beach, to the sand dunes; rock-pooling, making dens, building barbeques, playing adventure games, trying unsuccessfully to build rafts from driftwood. But as she got older these places evolved a new significance; they became places of sex and drink and dope. She'd avoided them. She'd left them to the hard kids and the holidaymakers. She had never had sex, *intercourse*. She had never done any rocking and rolling. The boys avoided her.

She looked at her friend's dreamy face. Julie had been with four boys, the first at fourteen, the fourth one was only a few weeks before. She had told Lauren about each of them in detail.

'Do you think he *likes* me?' Julie said, pulling a sequined pencil case out of her bag and unzipping it to pluck out a packet of mints.

'Hard to say.'

Lauren shook her head at the offered mint. She watched the sparkly pencil case go back into Julie's bag. Sitting in that tiny glittery case was a foil strip of pills, one of which Julie took every day. *I'm not getting pregnant, mate, I'm no fool!* This was true. Julie with her odd clothes and dramatic passions was no fool. That's why Lauren liked her.

'We were in Key Skills, last week? And he sat beside

me? He could have sat in at least three other places but he sat beside me!'

Lauren could not imagine Ryan and Julie as a couple. They just didn't fit. Ryan would end up with a female clone; expensive jeans and trainers and high-street tops, hoiked-up boobs and loads of gold jewellery. She might be black or she might be white but she would look like a hundred other girls.

'Hey, good-looking guy behind the counter!' Julie whispered, loud enough for the next table to hear.

She refused to look round so Julie started to talk about some of other kids at college. Lauren often wondered what they made of her. Although she was seventeen Julie said Lauren dressed like a ten-year-old tomboy. What that meant exactly she wasn't sure. She didn't have many clothes, they just weren't important to her. When she'd arrived in London she wore her jeans and boots and an array of oversize jumpers, their sleeves hanging over her wrists. As it got warmer she bought some shirts to wear over the jeans. She liked men's stuff, loose and baggy, the cuffs too long, covering her hands. She didn't have a skirt or dress. She didn't have any shoes with heels. Julie also said that her hair was *positively medieval. You're like Ophelia*, she'd said, showing her a picture of a painting by the artist Millais. A woman lying back in the water, her hair fanned out around her. She just laughed. She couldn't be bothered with it. Her hair was just *there*. Julie was constantly asking her if she could cut it, colour it, frizz it, or sculpt it. Julie, whose dress code was completely anarchic, said that Lauren was in dire need of a make-over. Lauren thought that might be one of her attractions for Julie. She saw the girl from Cornwall as a project.

'Look, look, the guy's coming this way!' Julie said in a whisper.

Lauren didn't bother to look. If it were an attractive guy he would most certainly be looking at Julie. She was like a great big blousy flower and Lauren was a humble daisy sitting in her shade.

'I know you. You're the girl who made me drop my onions.'

The voice came from behind. Lauren spun round. It was the guy with the starched apron. She turned back. She knew him. He'd had his hair cut very short and looked completely different in the café uniform but she knew him. It was the boy from 49 Hazelwood Road.

'Dropped his onions?' Julie said, a wicked look on her face. 'Is that some kind of code? Some sort of metaphor?'

Lauren looked away as he pulled out a chair and sat beside her. He was holding a cup of drink with a straw out of the top.

'We had a pedestrian collision and she made me drop my shopping. Then she wouldn't even tell me her name. How rude was that?'

'Oh dear, let me introduce you,' Julie said. 'This is Lauren Ashe from Cornwall. And I'm Julie Bell from the Roman Road.'

'Hi, Julie. Hi Lauren. I'm Nathan. Nathan Reddick,' he said.

'I have to go,' Julie said, standing up suddenly, giving Lauren a raised eyebrows look.

'I'm coming,' Lauren said.

'No, don't. You sit here while I go to the loo. I'll see you at the exit.'

Julie slid out from her seat and was gone in seconds. Nathan moved to where she had been sitting. Then he was staring straight at her. She looked away across the café but not before she'd noticed that his eyes were brown and his hair had flecks of grey at the front.

'Shouldn't you be working?' she said.

'My break.'

Lauren felt uncomfortable. It would be easy to get up and go. She didn't know him. She didn't owe him any politeness or courtesy. She pulled a strand of hair out of the tie at the back of her neck and began to play with it, winding it round her finger. After a few awkward moments she felt compelled to speak.

'So your onions were fine?'

He grinned suddenly showing almost every tooth he had. One of his front teeth had a chip at the bottom.

'Some needed counselling,' he said with a serious look.

For a second she was puzzled. Then, when the penny dropped, she laughed, her mouth opening in a wide smile. The laughter continued, tinkling out of her, unexpected. Nathan drank from his drink, a satisfied look on his face.

'Why were you looking at my house?'

'I wasn't,' she said, her face creasing.

'I was sure you were. Standing across the road, staring at it.'

'I was waiting for a lift. I was miles away. I didn't even notice your house. I was just staring into space.'

'Who was picking you up? Your boyfriend? Your dad?'

'My Uncle Donny. I live with him and my aunt. At least I used to.'

'Where'd do you live now?'

'I live with my aunt. It's my uncle who doesn't live there any more. It's complicated. Why are you giving me the third degree?'

'So, no boyfriend?'

'I didn't say that,' she said, relaxing again, now that they were off the subject of her old house.

'You do have a boyfriend?'

'I might,' she said.

'You should wear your hair loose,' he said.

'It's too long. It gets in the way.'

'If you wore it loose, you'd look like a mermaid. A mermaid from Cornwall.'

She laughed. He put his drink down on the table and his hand crept across the surface and lay on top of hers. He was so confident, so sure that she was bowled over by him. She ignored his hand and concentrated on the chip in his tooth. It was jagged and looked odd, like a cracked plate in the middle of a display of china.

'You'd like me. I'm multi-talented,' he said, his fingers making circles on the back of her hand, giving her a tingle that seemed to travel up her arm towards her chest.

She pulled her hand back and let it drop under the table.

'At what?' she said. 'Working in a café?'

'Just finished my gap year,' he said, sitting upright, as though he was about to stretch. 'I've been travelling. Europe, Asia, Australia. This is a summer job.'

'What about Cuba?' she said, folding her arms in front of her, 'Didn't you go there?'

'No.'

'You had a T-shirt on that said *Cuba*.'

'So, you did take some notice of me?'

He was staring at her again.

'I should go,' she said. 'I must find Julie. We have a class in about twenty minutes.'

'Give me your mobile number.'

'Julie'll be waiting,' she said, standing up, pushing her chair in to the table as if she were a pupil in a primary school class.

'Come round my house one night. I'll show you my travel photos.'

'That's an original line,' she smiled.

'49 Hazelwood Road. Come and see me Friday night. After seven. Just knock on the door. You know where it is.'

'I think I'm busy,' she said, turning away.

'I'll be waiting for you. Just after seven.'

She walked away towards the exit. Julie was outside; she could see a flash of pink and white. She headed towards her, passing the doll's house with the sign *Amy Miles' House 1890*. She paused for a moment and looked at the tiny figures. They were all frozen in one moment.

Part of her wanted to squat down and move them about like she used to do with her mum's doll's house. She walked on towards the exit and saw that Julie was talking to some boy.

*Come and see me.* Nathan Reddick's voice was there in her head.

Hazelwood Road. *You know where it is.*

# 7

On Friday evening Lauren sat at the computer to reply to a couple of emails from girls she'd known in St Agnes. She was glad to have something to do to take her mind off Nathan Reddick's invitation. She told herself that it had just been a casual invite. Probably he had forgotten it as soon as she left the museum. In any case how could she go to her old house? To Hazelwood Road? She just couldn't. It was out of the question.

And yet she couldn't help but think of him. She sat in front of the mirror and untied her hair. She let it hang down each side of her face. The ends of it lay across her breasts. She curled them round her fingers. Nathan had said she looked like a *mermaid*. It made her smile. She thought of the times she'd walked out of the sea at St Agnes with it dripping wet, stuck to her back, weighing her head down. Why hadn't she had it cut? Jessica had pleaded with her. *It's so difficult to manage!* she'd said, pulling the comb through it, trying not to hurt her, plaiting it tightly so that it was out of the way. When she undid the plaits her hair hung in waves.

Now she pulled it back from her face and tied it with an elastic grip at the back of her neck. At the front she clipped in a couple of Disney slides.

The sound of a door closing made her look round.

'I'm going out,' Jessica called out.

Lauren poked her head out into the hallway.

Jessica was dressed up. Lauren hadn't seen her looking like it for a long time. She had a new dress on, bright blue. It hung past her knees, the skirt full and flowing. Her legs were bare and she had heels on. Her hair had been washed and blow dried and she was wearing make-up, lipstick and mascara.

'Where are you going?'

'I'm going to see Donny. It's time for him and me to have a real chat. It's time for him to make a decision.'

'Did he call? Has something happened?'

'No, I've just made up my mind.'

'Oh, Jess, this is not the best thing to do.'

'I'm not waiting any more. I'm not hanging around in this dismal place just to see whether Donny eventually chooses me over his new woman. I've had enough. I have to know once and for all.'

'It's only been five or six weeks. We said we'd give him some time.'

'*You* said we'd give him time. Anyway the affair's been going on for months. Probably while we were in St Agnes. He's had time to decide who he wants. He's had plenty of time!'

She walked down the stairs, her bright blue dress flying out behind her. Lauren had a bad feeling in her chest.

'Wait, I'm coming,' she said, following her down,

pulling her jacket off the hallstand.

Jessica surged ahead up the street, turning the corner without pausing. Lauren was way behind wishing she was at home, at college, anywhere but on this journey with her aunt. It was hot, the sun heavy on the ground. She wished she hadn't bothered with her jacket. One of her shirt cuffs was tucked up inside the sleeve and she felt uncomfortable.

'Hang on, Jess,' she called, running and catching her up.

Jessica strode off and turned a corner without a second's hesitation, as if she already knew the way. Lauren wondered if she'd been round to Donny's new place before. Donny hadn't said anything the last time he came. A horrible thought occurred to her. Maybe Jessica had stood across the street from Donny's new home exactly as she had stood and watched the house in Hazelwood Road.

'Wait for me,' she said, quickening her step, a feeling of dismay propelling her on.

Donny's new home was in a small block of apartments alongside a canal. It was a modern building, the front of it mostly wood and metal tubing. It stood out among the red brick blocks of flats. Nearby were warehouses that had been cordoned off by fencing. There were signs announcing renovation, new gated apartments and health and fitness suites. Donny's building looked small and out of place. Lauren stood back from the doorway and wondered which floor he lived on. Jessica didn't pause as she hit one of the entry buttons. Leaning into the speaker she spoke rapidly and forcefully. A sharp buzz sounded and Jessica pushed the heavy glass entry door. Lauren quickly stepped in behind her.

They walked along a dark corridor to the back of the building as a door opened and Donny came out to meet them. Jessica paused and Lauren held her breath. There was something in the air, some sense of something about to happen; the heaviness of a hot day, the stuffiness of the corridor, the sense of being hemmed in. Could Jessica feel it? Her aunt's shoulders were still sharply back, her blue dress vibrant even in the shadowy innards of the building. Donny stood perfectly still as they approached. How easy it would be, Lauren thought, if he were to step forward and put his arms around Jessica. If he were to hug her tightly, to speak into her ear, to tell her he still loved her and was coming home, that these past months had been a stupid mistake, a life crisis, something he had to go through to show himself how much his family meant to him. Instead he stood to the side and invited her to go into the apartment. Lauren followed, feeling Donny's touch on her arm as she went by. In front of her Jessica seemed to stop unsure as where to go.

'Straight ahead,' Donny said, 'into the living room.'

They went into a smallish room with a sofa and a television and bookshelves. Jessica's heels sounded on the wooden floors and she walked across to the window and stood with her back to it.

'Have a seat,' Donny said.

She shook her head. The light from outside shone through her hair, the blue in her dress contrasting with her pale skin. Jessica had never looked so striking. Lauren sat down, perching on the edge of the sofa as far away from Donny as she could get. She wondered where his woman, Alison, was. She looked around the room. One wall was painted deep maroon. The others were pale cream. The sofa looked and felt new. Above the fireplace, on the mantle was a vase of flowers. Red roses. Tokens of love; Valentine flowers. Her eyes clung to them and it gave her a bad feeling about what Donny was going to say. She looked away, her gaze avoiding Donny or Jessica, and focused on the bookshelves. There, on the second shelf, was a small brown teddy bear with a tartan bow around its neck.

'I want you to come home,' Jessica said, breaking the uneasy quiet. 'We need you to come home.'

'Jessie, I can't. I've been through all this with you . . .'

'You think you're in love with this woman. I know that but if you were to come home, to come back just for a few days, a week, you'd see . . .'

'Jessie, I'm not coming back.'

'You owe us that,' Jessica said, her shoulders dropping, her hands bunching up the fabric of the dress and fiddling with it.

'Can I get you a cup of tea?' Donny said, clapping his hands together, as if they'd just arrived, as if nothing had yet been said. 'Or a cold drink?'

Without making any eye contact Lauren shook her

head. There was silence from Jessica.

'I'm glad you came because I was going to come and see you both this weekend.'

'Come home now. Come *home*!' Jessica said.

'I had something to tell you both.'

Lauren looked at the flowers and the teddy bear. Her insides twisted and she looked fearfully over at her aunt.

'Alison's going to have a baby.'

Jessica stared at Donny. Her mouth was a small dark hole. She seemed frozen against the window.

'I should say . . . *We* are going to have a baby. Alison and me.'

Lauren stood up and walked over to Jessica. She put her arm around her shoulder and whispered *We should go* in her ear. Her aunt's hair smelled of lemon.

'It was a surprise,' Donny continued, coughing slightly, putting his hand up, covering his mouth while he cleared his throat. 'We never expected anything to happen. Alison is thirty-nine. It's going to be a late baby.'

'You never wanted any babies,' Jessica said.

'That's true. When I was younger I didn't want . . .'

'You said we didn't need a baby. You said Lauren was enough for us!'

'That was true. She was.' He looked appealingly at Lauren. 'She is. For us. For us in *our* relationship. But with Alison and I . . .'

'You lied. If you'd wanted a baby you could have had one with me!'

Lauren was holding tightly onto Jessica's shoulder. She

felt her swaying, her anger building up. She tried to pull her away so that they could walk out of the room, out of the apartment but Jessica's weight seemed have sunk down into her legs pinioning her to the floor.

'It wasn't right for us. Not in our situation. We had Lolly,' Donny said, catching her eye, holding her attention while he continued. 'We simply didn't have the room. I don't mean in the house I mean in our lives. We put all our emotion into Lolly!'

'You liar,' Jessica said shrugging Lauren off, taking a step towards Donny. 'You liar, you liar!'

Lauren didn't know what to do. Then she heard a noise. Loud sobs. Big gasps of air inhaled and hiccupped back out again. When Donny and Jessica turned and looked at her she realised that she was crying. Her eyes were blurred with tears and her shoulders were shaking with emotion. She walked out of the room and along the hallway. In moments she was outside. The sound of heels on the ground behind her made her look round. Jessica was there.

They walked in silence, Lauren using the sleeve of her jacket to dry her face, to wipe her nose. After a few moments she had to say something.

'What did he mean? That you had no room for a baby? What did Donny mean?'

Jessica shook her head as if she didn't want to answer. She was striding out again moving in front of Lauren. Lauren put her hand out and caught her arm.

'What did he mean?'

'When we took you to Cornwall you'd just lost everything. You needed us, your family to be there for you. How could we have a new baby? Everything we did was for you. To help you get over your loss. Our loss. Everyone's loss. A new baby was a distraction. He said that. Those words came out of Donny's mouth. Not mine.'

'You didn't have a baby because of me?' Lauren said, puffing, trying to keep up.

'Don't say that,' Jessica said, grabbing her hand, squeezing it. '*You* were our baby.'

Jessica walked on but Lauren had stopped. In seconds her aunt had turned a corner. Maybe, when she realised that Lauren wasn't there with her, she would come back. Moment passed though and there was sign of her.

She waited anyway.

# 8

Hazelwood Road was a bus ride away but Lauren decided to walk. She didn't hurry. If Julie could see her now she would think she was going to meet Nathan. Maybe she was. Or maybe she was just walking a long circular route home to put off the time when she would have to face Jessica.

She approached Hazelwood Road from a different direction. It brought her to the other end of the street. She was surprised to see a small park there and then, in moments, it became familiar and she remembered it from her childhood. The sign said *Somers Park*. It had swings and a roundabout and a climbing frame that was shaped like a boat. She hesitated a moment then went in. There was no bench to sit on so she sat on the grass, cross-legged. She took her jacket off and laid it across her lap. It was gone six-thirty and there were groups of children in the play area clamouring over the boat climbing frame which looked new as though it had been recently replaced. Some teenagers had taken over the swing area and were sitting on the tiny swings. Other kids were hanging around in knots laughing and talking. Further out, on the field, there was a game of football going on.

Kids on bikes were cycling across the park even though there was a sign that said *No Bikes, Skateboards or Roller Skates*. As she watched she was aware of something forming in her head, a picture, a piece of moving film. A small child walking alongside a woman with a pushchair. The child was holding onto the handle. She had been told to *hold tight just in case*. It was her, Lauren Ashe, with her mother and her sister Daisy. *Can I go on the swings? They're too dangerous. I love the boat, can I climb on it? I'll be careful, honest I will. There are rough children there. I won't talk to them, Mummy. They'll knock you over. I'll run ahead, Mummy, to the pond. Come back, come back, you might fall into the water.*

Had there been a pond? Lauren sat upright, her back straight, and looked around. The park was rectangular and she could just see into the far corners. There'd been a pond over to the right, she was sure. A small area of water and rocks.

*Don't climb there, you might fall in!* Her mum's voice continued. All the while Daisy laid in her pushchair, her hands reaching out for brightly coloured figures that hung above her. They were made from different materials, some shiny, others crinkly, others in soft felt. One of them was a clown, its face made out of the whitest satin, its clothes vivid pink with blue dots. They all moved if touched and sometimes little bells rang. Mostly Daisy just laid there, her big eyes blinking up at the colours. Lauren loved to touch them, to trace their shape, to feel the fabrics, to rotate them. *Leave them, Lauren. You're blocking the light for the baby. Take care Lauren; you're knocking into the pushchair.*

A feeling of disgruntlement sat in her chest. Her memories of her mother and sister were so few that she didn't want to think of uncomfortable times, when she was being told off, when she felt unhappy or frustrated.

A ball rolled towards where she was sitting and a couple of young, red-faced boys puffed after it. She caught it and tossed it back to them. Then she got up and brushed the grass off her jeans and walked out of the park towards the turning for Hazelwood Road.

This end of the road was all houses and gardens, neater and more pretty than the other end where her house was. The first number she noticed was 293. It was a long road. She remembered walking along it, beside the pushchair, looking down at the pavement, watching her feet pass across the edges of the paving stones. The walk was quicker that way. Every ten steps or so she would look up and see the numbers pass; 249, 191, 172, 134. *Look where you are going, Lauren, you're walking too quickly. You'll trip up and pull the pushchair over with you!* Then they were there. Number 49. And yet wasn't there one day when her mum said the opposite? When the pushchair seemed to speed up and Lauren had trouble keeping up with it? As if they were all running away from something. Lauren remembered puffing, half running half walking, her mum saying *Hurry up! Hurry up!* The cloth figures on the pushchair were bouncing up and down, the clown in the middle seeming to dance happily. Then they were home, *Quick! Quick! Indoors!*

The memory stopped then, as if a door had shut in

her head and Lauren stood in front of her old house again. What was she doing there? Was she going to see this lad, this Nathan? Or was she only happy when she was hanging round this place. She half turned to go but then thought of Jessica, pacing up and down at home, her hands picking at her clothes. She pictured the blue dress lying in a heap at her feet and the cat turning delicate circles beneath her, the kittens meowing from the other room.

Donny was going to have a baby. The thought of it gave her an ache in her chest. During the ten years she'd been with them she'd never heard them talk about having a baby. It had never come up. Could it be that she had been the reason they had never had a child? Their own *blood* child? Now Donny had barely moved out of their house and he was buying teddy bears. *Lolly, you'll always be my girl* he had said but it wasn't true. He would have his own baby, a girl maybe and she would be his number one. And Jessica? How would she ever get over this? Lauren couldn't think of a single thing that she could say that would be a comfort.

She looked at her watch. It was just before seven. A couple of young women were walking along the pavement and she moved back out of their way. They were wearing skirt suits and one was talking non-stop and she heard the words *Promotion she said! Sideways move, more like!* And the other answered *Too right!* The heels of their shoes were scraping the pavement and she watched their neat shapes march up the road. Would she ever look like that she wondered? Would she ever *be* like that? Smart clothes, high heels, working in a bank or building society?

She looked down at her crumpled shirt over her jeans. Her plimsolls poked out, the laces tied in a double bow. One of the knees of her jeans was threadbare, would unravel any day. She should throw them away but they were her favourite pair.

She raised her eyes to the house. It looked blankly at her. Was anyone at home? The front garden area looked less cluttered. The wheelie bin was sitting untidily but the wood and the old cupboards had gone. She noticed then that the front door had changed. Instead of the shabby green door there was a half-glass wooden door with a brass knocker. It must have been put there recently because she could see some bright yellow curls of wood on the step which must have been shaved off to make it fit. Someone had been continuing the renovation. *Renovation*; to make new; rebirth. Was it possible to make this house new again? She knew it was. She'd watched programmes on television about people buying up old houses and giving them a make-over. Wooden floors, new lighting, fitted kitchen, new bathroom. She watched as people struggled to change the interior of a worn out house. Miracles had been performed. House hunters came in and were thrilled with the new ceilings and smooth walls, the downlighters and loft conversions.

But was it possible, in among this renovation, to strip out the memory of what had happened in this house?

She heard a window open from above and looked up.

It was the third floor, the attic window. Nathan's face was there. He made a pointing downwards gesture and disappeared. He was coming down to let her in. She felt herself tensing. Was she going to do this? To walk back into her old house? A few moments later the front door opened and he was standing there.

'I didn't think you'd come,' he said.

'I haven't come to see you,' she said, 'I've just been walking.'

'You look hot.'

'I've been wandering round for ages.'

She was hot. The walking and the upset had made her sweat. She was uncomfortable. Her hair felt heavy and damp at the back of her neck.

'Come in for a glass of water.'

He held the door open.

Would it hurt, to go in for a few minutes? Wasn't this what she'd really wanted, over the last weeks? Her visits to the street. Hadn't she wanted to go in and see what the house was like?

'Just for a glass of water,' she said.

She followed him into the house, one step at a time, not sure if she might suddenly turn tail and run back up the street.

'Hello!' a couple of voices called from further inside the house.

'Mum and Dad,' he explained.

She walked slowly along the hall. She'd been wrong about the banisters and the mosaic floor. The hallway was stripped back to wooden floorboards and the stairs were divided off by a fake wall. There was dust in the air, she could see it in the beam of light coming from the living room. She could even taste it. The kitchen door opened and two dogs bounded out. They were big, light-coloured; retrievers she thought, their hair flying out as they approached her.

'This is Prince and this is Duke,' Nathan said, squatting down to pat both the dogs at the same time.

'Royalty,' she said, reaching out to touch the ears of the nearest one. 'We have some kittens and we've named them after queens; Victoria, Alexandra and Juliana.'

'That's a mouthful for a tiny kitten,' a female voice said.

A tall, thin lady was standing in the kitchen door. She had heavy black glasses on and a skirt that went all the way down to the ground. She was holding a small china cup and drinking in from it.

'We don't use their full names any more. It's Vicky, Alex and Jules. We do call the mother by her full name, Cleopatra.'

She was talking too much. What did anyone care about the names of her cats?

'I'm just getting Lauren a drink,' Nathan said, walking ahead, into the kitchen. 'Oh, this is Lauren, Mum. Lauren this is Karen, my mum. My dad's in here.'

Lauren smiled awkwardly, feeling her fingers being nibbled by one of the dogs.

Nathan's dad was sitting at the kitchen table, a newspaper spread out in front of him. He looked up and gave her a smile. He was wearing working clothes, a paint-spattered T-shirt and washed-out cotton trousers. He was doing a crossword. As she waited for her drink she noticed him filling in a clue and then pushing his pen behind his ear as he sat back and drank from a glass of orange.

Nathan's mum was talking about the work they were doing on the house. She was describing how they'd had to rip three the flats out in order to make it back into one residence. Lauren nodded and looked interested. All the while she was looking round the kitchen. It bore no resemblance to anything she remembered. Everything in it was glowing. The cupboard doors were like mirrors, the worktops were glossy, the fridge was stainless steel. She could only vaguely recall what it had been like when she'd lived there. There'd been units she was sure and a fridge with a freezer at the bottom. They'd had checked curtains she remembered. Red and white. Nathan handed her a glass of water with ice and a slice of lemon in it.

'This room is nice,' she said.

'This is the only finished room. I said to Tony, I don't mind the rest of the house being a building site but I must have my kitchen!'

She heard Nathan tell his mum to stop going on and then he took her by the shoulder and manoeuvred her out of the kitchen door. The dogs followed them along the hallway. Lauren was still drinking from her glass. She stood by the front door and gulped it down, the cold liquid going down the back of her throat. Nathan had one foot on the bottom stair.

'You could come up to my room for an hour. Just to sit down, have a rest. I've got my travel photos on my laptop?'

'I should go,' she said.

'It's early though. Just come up for half an hour?'

He walked up a couple of stairs. She held the empty glass out. She wasn't quite sure what to do with it. She placed it on the hall table and then looked at the front door. With two or three steps she could walk out onto the street. In minutes she would be at the end of the road, at her bus stop. She'd seen the inside of the house. Was there any point in staying longer?

'My room's in the attic. It gives you an aerial view for miles. Well, half a mile maybe. People would gladly pay to come up and see it.'

She gave a tiny smile.

'Just for ten minutes?'

She hesitated. She could step towards him or she could back away and leave. It was her choice.

'Come on,' he said, his voice silky.

She walked towards the stairs.

# 9

She followed Nathan. She allowed the distance between them to lengthen so that when he got to the top she wasn't even halfway. When she got to the landing the floor looked odd. Part of it was floorboards and part of it was carpeted. She could see a furrow where a wall had once been presumably to divide off the middle floor flat. It had been taken down but still its presence seemed tangible, the area inside it painted a pinkish white. The remaining landing would have been just wide enough for one person. She moved along it avoiding looking directly at the door that had once been her parents' bedroom. She felt disoriented. It didn't seem like being in her old house. But then she had no idea what that really would have felt like. Her memories of this house were those of a seven-year-old child.

Then she had spent a lot of time in her parents' bedroom. She remembered the big silky bed and giant furniture, a wardrobe and chest of drawers that took up most of one wall. The doll's house that had always been the focal point for her. As soon as she entered the room she would look at it covetously, her hands itching to play with it. Her own room had been smaller, painted pink with a border of purple balloons right round the wall from one edge of the door to the other. Across the floor were all the things she owned; her soft toys and miniature desk and chair, her books and games. In the corner was her own doll's house bought for her by her mum one Christmas. It was made out of plain, thin wood, with just four rooms and silly furniture. The figures looked like *dolls* not people.

Daisy had slept in the cot in her mum's room.

'Are you coming?'

She heard Nathan's voice from the middle of the second flight of stairs. She moved on and turned into the stairwell. She paused for a second, aware that this part of the house had not changed. The narrow, dark, staircase up to the attic. She went up a couple of steps as Nathan reached the top. He pulled the attic door open and a bright slab of light fell onto the top few steps. When she got into the room she saw why. The front of the room had remained the same. It had a small window which looked out on to the street. The back of the room had been transformed with a dormer window. It was more spacious and she could see acres of sky.

'Wow,' she said, puffing lightly after the stairs.

'This *had* to be my room,' Nathan said.

When she had lived in the house it had been where Jessica slept.

She looked around it now. On one side there was a single bed and some bookshelves. On the other side was a rail which was crammed full of clothes. The dormer window had some big cushions underneath. The desk by the small attic window had a laptop on it. The screen saver showed the two dogs, one sitting upright, the other lying down, both facing the camera, their honey-coloured hair mingling.

'It's nice in here,' she said, suddenly feeling awkward.

He was standing grinning at her. She pulled a strand of her hair out and twisted it round her finger.

'I like the way you do that, playing with your hair. It's a defence mechanism.'

She went to speak but before she could say a word he leaned towards her and kissed her on the mouth. Her eyes were open and she was surprised but the kiss only took a few seconds and then he backed away.

'I wanted to get that over with,' he said.

She was puzzled and put her fingers up to her mouth.

'I mean I *wanted* to kiss you. I've wanted to kiss you since the day you barged into me but that wasn't the right time. What with . . .'

'The onions . . .'

'Right. So then I wanted to kiss you in the museum but it was too public.'

'And you may have got sacked.'

'True. Kissing the customers is definitely frowned on—'

He stopped and looked as though he was considering something.

'And then tonight,' he said. 'As soon as you came into my house I wanted to kiss you but I had to pick the right moment.'

'Now is the right moment?'

'I couldn't do it in front of my mum and dad. And I couldn't pounce on you the moment I got you out of the kitchen. It might have upset the dogs. And on the stairs, that might have seemed predatory.'

She was having trouble keeping a straight face. He was always using long words. *Predatory*, it made him sound like a prowling beast.

'When we got up here I decided I had to do it. I had to break the tension between us.'

'I don't feel any tension,' she said, with a small smile.

'I do, though.'

He was looking straight at her and his arms were hanging down awkwardly as if he didn't know what to do with them. Then, when she didn't answer, he folded them across his chest. *Defence mechanism*, she thought. She raised one hand and touched his cheek. Then she moved up towards him, closed her eyes and brushed her lips against his. After a few seconds she pushed harder, opening her mouth. She felt him tense then relax and his arms dropped and circled her waist. Then she pulled back and stood up straight. He let his arms drop away from her.

'How's that?' she said. 'Does that feel any better?'

'Much better,' he said. 'Now come and look at my photos.'

She sat down in front of his laptop. He pulled out a fold-up chair from behind the clothes rail and set it up next to her. He was talking all the time about his digital camera, about how he had to ration his pictures.

He could have taken a photograph every ten minutes, he said, there was so much to see in Australia. Still talking, he nudged the mouse. The screen changed and she was faced with what looked like the front page of a newspaper.

**House of Death** *Mother and child murdered in Hazelwood Road. Seven-year-old survives carnage.*

'I'll get rid of this,' Nathan said.

It took a moment to register what she was seeing. The words were shocking enough but in the middle of the page was a photograph of her mum. A smiling picture from years before.

'I'll shut it down,' he said, moving the mouse and clicking it shut.

She moved her chair back as if to get up but her eyes were glued to the screen. He turned to her and looked puzzled, his forehead crinkling.

'It's just something I'm researching. Sorry, has it upset you?'

'Open it up,' she said.

'Not if it will upset you.'

'Please, open it up,' she said.

He opened the document and the newspaper page was in front of her. She looked at the headline, at the words, at the photograph of her mum. Underneath it the caption read *Grace Slater, 35-year-old mother of two.* She felt her breath stop and looked at her mum's pretty face. Jessica said that Lauren looked like her, that she had the same mouth and eyes but Lauren couldn't see it. What she saw was a serious looking lady with smart hair and hoop earrings.

'I'll close it down,' Nathan said and the screen changed again.

She stood up. 'I should go,' she said.

'I've spooked you. I shouldn't have left this on the screen. This house has a dark past. I didn't think to mention it. You don't do you? You don't tell people who come into your house what happened there years before. I should have shut it down but I was looking out of the window waiting for you. When I saw you come along I thought I'd better get down there quickly in case you went.'

She stared at him, her face stiff.

'This house – this house that my mum and dad bought at auction – it has a terrible past. There was a murder here. That's why it was turned into flats. Mum and dad emailed me about it when I was abroad? They wanted to make sure I was all right with living in a house where something bad had happened.'

'And you are?'

'Yes. I mean obviously I wish it hadn't happened at all but I'm all right living here. Look, maybe I shouldn't tell you any more. It's a bit squeamish. But it didn't happen here, in *this* room. It was downstairs in the main bedroom.'

She knew that. This room hadn't been big enough to swing a cat in in those days. She knew that better than him.

'This man killed his family here. It was downstairs. My mum and dad accept it.'

'I really do have to go,' she said, pushing the chair back, standing up, 'It's getting late.'

'It's a horrible story. Maybe I shouldn't have told you. It was ten years ago. People die in houses all the time.'

'What I don't get is why you're *researching* it.'

'Because if I know everything that happened then I can come to terms with it. If I think there's hidden stuff it will make me feel uneasy.'

She nodded. It sounded like a sensible approach. How easy it was for him.

'I'm sorry. I can't think what to say. It's just the history of this house. I 'spose I think the more I tell it the less awful it sounds.'

'I just have to go.'

In seconds she was walking down the narrow stairs. She could hear him coming behind her. For once he was quiet. Along the landing she stood still for a second putting her jacket on even though it wasn't cold. She did the buttons up right to the top as she looked at the door of her parents' old bedroom. It was white. When she'd lived there it had been wood, she was sure. Come to think of it everywhere had been stripped wood. Her father liked everything to look natural. She remembered that.

Nathan was behind her.

'Mum and Dad told me about it before they bid for the house. They were worried that I might feel uncomfortable. But, it's history, you know. Every house has history; births, deaths, happiness, sadness.'

'I need to get home. My aunt's not well,' she said and walked on down the main stairs.

Immediately the dogs were in front of her, their tails wagging in unison, their tongues hanging out. She let her hands ruffle their fur and then walked to the front door. From the kitchen she could hear the sound of jazzy music.

'Will you come again? No, stupid question. Not now that I've spooked you you'll never come here again.'

She heard a beep and took her mobile out. The name *Jessica* was on the screen.

'Look,' Nathan said, looking flustered and upset, 'will you at least let me give you my mobile number?'

He was upset. His short hair made him look older, less boyish. She felt sorry for him. He wasn't to know. She handed him her mobile. He took it solemnly and began to key in his number. When he finished he handed it back to her.

'Do you know who died here?' she said.

'Two people. A woman and her baby. Another child survived.'

She nodded.

'Will you ring me?'

'Maybe,' she said, opening the door and going out past the wheelie bin and into the street.

*I need to know everything*, he'd said. Would he really like to know what had happened here in this house?

One morning, when she was seven, she woke up in her

mother's bed. On the other side of the bed lay Daisy who was dead. Across the room, slumped in the space between the giant wardrobe and the chest of drawers, was her mother. She was paler and stiller than Lauren had ever seen her. In her chest was a deep wound.

The only other person in the room was her father, Robert Slater.

# 10

Jessica wanted to go back to Cornwall. The decision took only days to finalise. Lauren didn't try and argue her out of it. For the first time in months and certainly since the day at Donny's flat Jessica looked bright and energetic. For five days she talked around the subject. They could pack up and go back together. They could hire a van. There wasn't that much that really belonged to them at the flat, just clothes, personal stuff; some ornaments, bedding and linen. They would get summer jobs, maybe decorate the house. It would be painful, being there without Donny, but their old friends were around, the people and places they knew. The holidaymakers were a nuisance but still it was a chance to make a bit of money and it would keep them busy. There would be no time to sit and mope.

Jessica virtually sang out the words. It was an escape plan. A way of tunnelling out of the dark place she found herself in. There was one thing they absolutely had to buy and that was a decent sized pet-carrier for the cat and the kittens. They had to come. Their life was with Jessica and Lauren. They would settle. The city cat who had adopted them months before would acclimatize itself and become a seaside cat. Jessica fussed over them and in a silly high voice told them all about St Agnes, calling them by their full regal names. Now and then she picked up one of the kittens and cradled it using her finger to touch its tongue. It made Lauren shiver. Cats had sandpaper tongues and it always made her feel quivery when they tried to lick her. She watched while Jessica whispered sweet nothings to the kittens, the mother cat looking anxiously on from the corner.

All through these conversations Jessica talked about the importance of secrecy. *I don't want Donny to know. I want him to come here and find that we've gone. I want him to be shocked.*

Lauren pictured the scene. Donny would park his car outside the flat, leave his new briefcase on the passenger seat and come up to the front door. He would ring the bell out of politeness but when no one answered he would use his own key and walk in, calling out to Jessica. There would be no answer though, no lights anywhere, no smell of toast or coffee or washing powder; no sound of the telly or the distant radio in the bathroom; no sign of movement or life.

Would Donny feel the sense of loss? Would his footsteps echo around the house, each room staring emptily back at him?

It wouldn't happen though. The house wouldn't be empty because, as Lauren told Jessica over and over again, *she* couldn't go back to Cornwall yet. She'd already moved college once that year and couldn't do so until her exams were over. Then she would go back and do the second year of her 'A' levels there.

But Jessica couldn't wait three weeks. It seemed as though she couldn't wait three days.

Jessica had to go on, alone. Lauren explained it gently, over and over again. She would stay in the house and finish her year at college. She was in the middle of her preparation for the Art exam which was to take eight hours. Her bedroom was littered with sketches of doll's houses and collages of figures and furniture and fabrics that she was using to prepare for the final exam. Then there was the Drama performance and the History paper.

Jessica became anxious. How could she leave Lauren to look after herself, to live alone? What sort of responsible adult would do that? But those words meant nothing because Jessica knew that Lauren had been looking after the both of them for weeks, ever since Donny had left.

*I can do this!* Lauren had said, many times. *I'll email, I'll phone every day. Let me do my exams. The three weeks will whiz by. I'll be back in St Agnes before you know it.*

It was decided. Jessica would hire a van and take most of their stuff back to Cornwall. Lauren would live in the flat until her exams were over. Then she would join her.

On Thursday Lauren walked out of college and saw Nathan standing across the road. It made her stop. She raised her hand in a wave.

She'd been in the Drama studio all afternoon and the noise of students working had given her the beginnings of a headache. Seeing him was a total surprise and she wanted to smile. Underneath though there was still the uncomfortable feeling of seeing all that stuff on his laptop.

She cut through the traffic and in moments was standing in front of him.

'How do you know this is my college?'

'There's only one college in this area. I didn't have to be Sherlock Holmes to work it out,' he said giving only a hint of a smile at his own joke.

'What are you doing here?'

'I wanted to talk to you. After last week. After being in my house. There's something I wanted to say. Look, my car's round the corner, I could give you a lift home.'

'You don't have to worry. Forget about it. It was nothing.'

'I can't forget about it. I know about you . . .'

'What?' she laughed, looking round, a little self-conscious, hoping that Julie wouldn't appear from somewhere.

'I know about you and your family. I know who you are.'

'I don't get you.'

'Lauren Ashe,' he said, lowering his voice, 'From Cornwall. You used to live in my house. Ten years ago . . .'

She sighed. She could feel her headache growing.

'I supposed you looked me up on your computer,' she said, rubbing her forehead with her knuckles.

'No. My mum was talking to a neighbour. She said that she'd spoken to the girl who used to live in our house.'

'Oh,' she said.

She pictured Molly. The twins came into her head. Two ten-year-old girls who looked identical.

'Let me give you a lift home,' he said.

She stood for a moment not knowing what to do. Some kids she knew edged past her. Across the road, in among the crowds coming out of college she thought she could see a white-blonde head. The last thing she wanted was for Julie to see her talking to Nathan. Especially now at this very moment.

'All right. I live near the London Hospital.'

She followed him round the corner to a black hatchback car. She got into the passenger seat. The foot area was cluttered with debris, half full plastic bottles of water, newspapers and a couple of empty sandwich triangles.

'Sorry,' Nathan said, leaning across, scooping up some of the mess and putting it behind his seat, 'this car's a tip.'

'Is it yours?' Lauren said.

'Mum gave it to me. I think that's why I let it get into a mess. A little bit of silent rebellion.'

Lauren fitted her feet in between the remaining clutter.

'Dad started teaching me to drive on my seventeenth birthday,' he said as if she'd asked.

He started up the car. Loud music came on immediately and he turned it off.

'I'm sorry about last week, about you seeing that stuff on the laptop. If I'd known . . .'

'It's all right,' she said. 'How could you have known? There's nothing for you to apologise for!'

Her voice was light, upbeat. She didn't feel like that though. They stopped at some lights and a wave of schoolchildren in dark uniforms crossed in front of them. She was impatient for them to pass. But even though the lights had changed to green they still had to wait for the last stragglers to get across.

'Was that why you were looking at the house? That first night I saw you?' he said, his voice tentative.

'No!' she said. 'Why won't you believe me? I was waiting for a lift.'

It was awkward. None of her friends had ever known about her family. They just knew her as Lauren Ashe, living with her aunt and her boyfriend. They just accepted the story that her mum and dad had died in a car crash. That was that.

'I talked to my mum and dad about it. I hope you don't mind.'

She shrugged her shoulders, a feeling of irritation growing inside her. His mum and dad knew. How many other people would he tell?

'My mum said that you're very welcome to come round. To look round the house. If you wanted to. If that would help . . .'

'It's the next right turn,' she said.

'My dad worked as a social worker for some years. He said that it's sometimes cathartic to revisit the scene of a crime.'

'*Cathartic*? What does that mean?' she said, jokily, even though she knew.

'Getting rid of troublesome feelings,' he said, as though he'd just memorised a dictionary definition.

'Pull over here,' she said.

The car stopped.

'It's very nice of your parents to be concerned but I don't have any troublesome feelings about the house, *your* house. Last week, it was just a shock to see the old reports on your computer. You have to remember that I never saw any of it at the time. It's been ten years. I've come to terms with it.'

She opened the door.

'Can I see you again?' he said.

'I'm really busy at the moment with my exams. Can I give you a call? I've got your number.'

She closed the car door and walked away. She heard him get out of the car.

'You know what they say about mermaids?' he shouted.

She turned back to him.

'That mortals should never get involved with them.'

'Did you find that on the internet?' she said.

He nodded, a wry, defeated expression on his face.

'I'll call you,' she said.

The next day Jessica was leaving. The pet-carrier was bought and the van was hired and packed. She took a last look around the house checking in drawers and cupboards to make sure she'd not left anything behind.

She came into Lauren's room holding a top of Donny's.

'I found this under the bed. Shows how often I cleaned there,' she said sitting down on Lauren's bed.

'It's old.'

Jessica handed it to her. There was writing across the chest. The word *Florida* was in italics and had faded. Donny had never been to Florida but got the T-shirt in a sale. Lauren was reminded of the one that Nathan had been wearing on the day she'd first bumped into him in Hazelwood Road. The word *Cuba* had been emblazoned across it and yet he'd never been there either.

'Keep it, you could use it as a duster,' Jessica said, letting it drop onto the duvet.

Lauren picked it up. Jessica looked around the wall at some of the sketches that Lauren had stuck there.

'Doll's houses,' Jessica said.

'What about them?'

'Your mum loved that old doll's house. She treasured it.'

There was quiet in the room. Lauren didn't know how to answer. Jessica never spoke about her mum or anything to do with the house on Hazelwood Road.

'She tried to get me to play with it but I always thought it was a bit creepy.'

'I loved playing with it,' Lauren said.

'When I was very young, about five, six, seven, I think and she was a grown-up teenager, about your age, she used to make up little games around it. She'd say, *Today we're spring cleaning the bedrooms* or *We're going to help make some cakes for the family*. Or she might hide a ten pence piece in there somewhere, under a table of behind one of the dolls and tell me I had to find it. Like a game of hide and seek. I think she was hoping to trigger some interest in me.'

Jessica stopped for a moment. Lauren sensed that she was still thinking about it. She didn't fill the silence, she wanted Jessica to go on talking about her mum.

'She used to write me these notes. When I came in from school she'd say, *The postman left you a letter in the doll's house*. And I'd go up to her room, open the front of the dusty old thing and there, sat in between the chair and the table, was a tiny letter addressed to Miss Jessica Ashe. She did all those things just to make me like it. Then one day she stopped. She must have realised that I didn't want to play with it.'

'What happened then?'

'She took me out on my bike. Much more fun than playing with some old antique.'

Jessica looked at the T-shirt that was in Lauren's hands. She took a corner of it and pulled at it gently.

'Everything changes, everything moves on. Like this house. Poky little place. Not much bigger than a doll's house. I thought we were going to have a new life here, a fresh start. Now I'm leaving.'

'A fresh start? Did you and Donny need a fresh start?'

Jessica nodded and tears came into her eyes. She bunched up the T-shirt and held it to her face. Lauren could just see part of the word *Florida*.

'If I'm honest, things weren't that great down in St

Agnes. We thought that if Donny got a new job then it would make everything better. But it wasn't to be.'

Lauren slipped her arm through Jessica's. She waited for the sobs or the bitter words but neither came. Jessica seemed calmer than she had been in months.

'I think I'll take this back to St Agnes with me,' she said holding the T-shirt.

The van was packed by nine. The cats were the last to go in.

'It's a long drive,' Lauren said, feeling oddly strange standing on the pavement, watching Jessica fitting the pet-carrier in next to her packed bags.

'I'll stop halfway for a break. There shouldn't be too much traffic. It's not Saturday.'

Lauren nodded. Jessica came close and put her arms around her.

'You'll be all right? You know, worst comes to the worst you can call on Donny. If a fuse blows or you need a plumber.'

'I can fix a fuse,' Lauren said, 'I'm not hopeless.'

'I know. Meanwhile I'll get me and the cats settled in the house and ask around for summer work. You'll see, we'll fit back in. It'll be as though we'd never left.'

Jessica hugged her tightly. After a few moments she let her go. When she stood back Lauren could see that Jessica's face was reddening as if she was about to burst into tears.

'Three weeks,' she said, 'It's just three weeks.'

Jessica nodded and got into the van. A few seconds later the engine started and it drove off. Lauren stood watching it until it reached the corner. She waved enthusiastically, her arm up high. Even when it turned out of the street she continued for a few moments. She must have looked stupid but she didn't care.

# Part Two

# House of Memories

# 11

Living alone was a guilty relief. She wasn't constantly worrying about Jessica and her emotional state. After weeks of tiptoeing around the house she was able to relax. Donny and Jessica; Jessica and Donny. They were both gone and although Lauren missed them in different ways she felt the heaviness of their break-up slip off her shoulders.

She didn't have to tidy up. She could leave things out and not worry about anyone complaining. If she didn't feel like washing up after a snack then she left the dishes on the side. Her bed stayed unmade for days as she dashed off to college. The towels in the bathroom hung damply over the side of the bath, her toiletries laid here and there. The toilet roll sat on the window sill instead of hooked onto its holder.

The first week was full of sleep and work and revision. The house became a bit like an obstacle course. The living-room floor was littered with scatter cushions and her books and papers and empty glasses. In the kitchen most of the dishes were washed but left on the side in piles along with cereal packets and jam and packets of pasta and sauce. There was no point in putting them away to take them out again hours later.

She was busy. Her Art work had to be finished and she spent hours prepping it and deciding which sketches and plans to work on. The Drama coursework was finished but there was still work to be done for History.

Every night she phoned Jessica and wrote emails when she had a minute. She was glad to have a lot to do. It made the days slide by.

She thought of Nathan from time to time. She pictured him standing by his car as she walked away the previous week. He liked her she knew. When she first met him she had been flattered by his interest. Now that he knew her story she felt troubled every time she thought of him. As if he was now a part of that gloomy bit of her life.

She got on with her work. There was no point in thinking about him. She was going back to Cornwall. There couldn't be any relationship between them even if she wanted it.

One day she paused as she came back from college into the hallway. There were letters on the mat and as she picked them up she found herself staring at the hall stand. It was empty and looked odd. When they'd first lived there it had been covered in coats; Donny's jacket and his long wool coat; Jessica's puffa jacket and Lauren's Parka and walking coat. Sometimes it had been so full up that nothing else would fit on it. Later in the winter these things had been replaced with lighter jackets and sweatshirts. Now there was nothing hanging there, not even an umbrella. It seemed abandoned. Even Lauren's denim jacket was upstairs lying on her bed.

It was thin and bare, like a tree that had lost its leaves.

She placed the letters on the side and trudged into the living room. The place was a mess. Donny would have hated it. He would have rushed round picking things up; dishes first, rubbish in a bin bag and cushions and magazines back where they belonged. Even Jessica would have tutted and tidied up. Lauren had no energy though. She sat down heavily on the sofa and stared at the glass screen of the television. She had two weeks to go until she went back to St Agnes. It seemed like two months.

She finally told Julie Bell about being on her own. They were in one of the Art rooms and Julie was putting together some sketches for her three dimensional sculpture. It wasn't a particularly warm day but Julie was wearing a strapless top. Her milky-white shoulders were plump and rounded, a tiny bird tattooed on the top of one of her arms. She had a black band on her hair and the end of it hung down her back.

'Come and stay at my house. We've got loads of room,' she said, her eye travelling up and down Lauren's baggy clothes.

'I like my own space.'

'But you could come for a sleepover! Or even better Ryan and I could come over to you. What about Saturday? I've got some frozen vodka.'

Ryan had finally become Julie's boyfriend. Lauren had seen the two of them around college, whispering in corners.

'It's the weekend before the first exam.'

'So what? It'll relax us. Last minute revision is never a good thing. Hey! I could bring Ryan's mate, Dexy. He's nice.'

'*Dexy?*' Lauren said.

'His real name is Lawrence Dexter. He prefers Dexy.'

'I don't know.'

Lauren couldn't imagine such an evening.

'I know! You're seeing that kid. That Nathan,' Julie said.

'I'm not!'

'Have you slept with him yet?'

Lauren's mouth dropped open.

'Don't look like that. That's what relationships are all about.'

'Not always. They're about other things. Friendship, trust, loyalty.'

Julie opened her mouth in a fake yawn.

'You're not seeing him, then.'

Lauren didn't answer.

'I'll bring the vodka over. Saturday. About nine. You'll like Dexy. He's not as nice as Ryan but still . . .'

Lauren didn't argue. Giving in to Julie was always easier.

When she got home on Thursday there were two letters. One was junk mail. The second was addressed to her. *Miss Lauren Ashe*. The envelope was thick and expensive and in the top left-hand corner was the name of the sender; Barrat and Morris Solicitors. A feeling of gloom settled on her. Legal correspondence had only ever been about one subject. She tore open the white envelope. The words, *Dear Miss Ashe* were followed by the name of her father, in bold and underlined, **Robert Slater**.

It was a letter from her father's solicitors.

Why couldn't he just leave her alone?

# 12

She cooked some pasta and mixed it with sauce. She didn't sit at the table but leaned against the units and ate forkfuls of the food straight out of the pot. She surveyed the kitchen table. On it were the letters that her father had sent her over the years. The pink plastic folder that had held them sat on the one of the chairs. The surface of the table was tidy, the letters neatly in small piles. She ate the pasta while staring at them, her eye flitting from pile to pile.

There were a large number from the early years when her father had first gone to prison and then they gradually tailed off until the present year when there had been just one. The letter that Donny had given her some weeks back, sent to him at his old school and forwarded. Before cooking she'd counted them. Sixty-three letters that spanned ten years.

The solicitor's letter sat on the work surface close to where she was eating. She glanced at it from time to time. She ate for a while longer and then took the pot over to the sink and washed it. Then she picked up the solicitor's letter and re read it.

*Dear Miss Ashe,* it read, followed by her father's

name in bold. *We have been appointed as the legal representatives of your father, Robert Slater. His second appeal is scheduled to be heard in the High Court in early September. He has been informed that you are now domiciled in the London area and is concerned about the surrounding publicity of his case and how it may affect you. He has instructed us to contact you and inform you of the circumstances of his appeal.*

*You may, or may not be aware, that your father is eligible for a parole hearing. In effect this could mean early release. This could only happen if your father were to admit his guilt. However he has never done this and says he never would. Your father has always maintained his innocence. This means he has to stay in prison until the completion of his sentence or until an appeal court sets aside the verdict of his first trial.*

*Notwithstanding the importance of this appeal your father is resolute that you should not be upset by his attempts to prove his innocence. It is for this reason that he is keen that you should be made aware of the nature of his appeal in September.*

*To this effect we would be happy to meet at your convenience. If you could telephone and make an appointment it would be much appreciated.*

The letter was signed by *Ms Rachel Morris.*

She put it down. She would be back in Cornwall in September.

She washed up and then sat down at the kitchen table in front of the other letters. She sighed, letting her fingers run across them. Then she started to take them out of their envelopes.

The early ones were short, just one side of a page.

They were written in large script, easy perhaps for a seven-, eight-, or nine-year-old to read. As time went on and the letters became less frequent the script got smaller and the content lengthened. Had her father imagined her growing and becoming more mature, more able to follow two sides of A4, line after line of closely written words, the handwriting becoming more slanted in some. When she got to the last four letters, written over recent years, she saw that they had been printed out by a computer.

She read them all. She didn't think of the time or the other things she had to do, she just read each one from beginning to end and then went on to the next one. When she finished she sat back. It was dark outside and she saw that it was almost ten. She stretched her arms out straight, her joints cracking. Then she flipped through the papers on the table and picked up the first ever letter and re-read it quickly, a dozen lines, no more. *I hope you are well . . . I miss you very much . . . There's been a terrible mistake . . . Your poor mum and sister Daisy . . . I love you . . . I don't blame you . . .* She threw it down without finishing it.

Another one caught her eye. It had been written the first Christmas that her father had spent in prison. At the top of each corner he had drawn two small Christmas trees. *Dear Lauren, I hope Father Christmas brings you lots of things and that you have a good time by the seaside with Aunty Jessica and Uncle Donny. I am keeping well and longing to see you some time when this whole terrible mess has been sorted out. Remember that your old dad's thinking about you all the time. I don't blame you for what you said in court. You just told the truth. I understand that. When you are older you will understand that sometimes the things we see are not always what they seem. I love you. Happy Christmas! Dad.*

She felt a sudden sharpness in her throat. *I don't blame you.* Why did he keep saying that? How could he blame her?

She stood up and turned her back on the letters. She turned off the light in the kitchen and went up to the bathroom to have a shower. After a while of trying to read through some of her notes she got into bed and tried to sleep.

She woke early. The light edged through the sides of the blind. She looked at her clock. It showed 05:19. She thought of getting up, doing some reading or essay practice. She sat up. She'd wasted the previous evening reading her father's letters. She should do some work. She was on the brink of throwing back the covers and getting out of bed when she suddenly felt overwhelmed with tiredness. She lay back and stared at the ceiling. Her eyes were open but her mind floated elsewhere, onto another bed, in another house ten years before.

It was very early in the morning when Lauren woke up. She'd gotten used to sleeping in her mum's big bed. The duvet cover was silky and she liked the feel of it rubbing against her skin. There was loads of room as well. Even though her mum slept next to her she felt as if she could stretch her legs and arms without touching anything. The only thing she didn't like was having to be so quiet all the time *in case Daisy wakes up*. Daisy, who, during the day, could sleep through the loudest television programme, had super hearing powers when night time came. A single whisper could jolt her awake. So Lauren kept her thoughts to herself. If she woke up early she simply got up, crept over to the doll's house and looked in through the windows at the tiny figures in the rooms. It wasn't possible to open it without making a noise so she just sat and made up a story about what was happening inside.

This morning though she felt too tired to get up and start playing.

Maybe it was because she'd been unwell. It made her feel sleepy. In fact she felt as if she were half asleep and half awake. Her eyelids felt heavy and sticky, as if she couldn't actually open them if she wanted to. She tried to move her arm but it seemed to weigh an enormous amount. She had an idea that her mother had got up. And yet there was something there beside her. The smell of the bed was different. A baby smell. Daisy was in bed with her instead of her mum. She quietened her breathing and lay thinking about it. Why was Daisy lying there and not in her cot?

There was a sound from outside in the street. A car door banging. Then it was quiet again. But when she listened hard she realised that there were birds singing. Lots of them, their chirps cutting across each other. They sounded happy and busy as if they had loads to do and were looking forward to the day.

She tried to open her eyes and thought she had but it was still dark. Then she realised that somehow one of the pillows was over head. She moved her arm and edged it to the side. Then it was light and she saw that she was on her back looking at the ceiling. She turned her head and saw Daisy lying on the other side of the big bed. Strangely, one of her mum's pillows seemed to be resting across Daisy's face. Lauren knew she should reach over and move it but it was such an effort and she was so tired. It felt as though it was late at night, past twelve o'clock and yet the room was flooded with daylight.

She wondered where Mum was.

There was a noise from downstairs. The sound of footsteps walking around, each step echoing on the floorboards. It was as though someone was cross and in a hurry. Then it was quiet for a while and she must have drifted back into the half sleep that she'd been in before.

She opened her eyes again. The footsteps were coming up the stairs. Something about them was making her feel uneasy. She moved her hand and felt the space where her mum usually lay. It was cold and empty. If she stretched her arm further she could just touch Daisy.

Where was her mum? Was it just Lauren and Daisy in the big bed?

The footsteps were on the landing. They were louder than before but they'd slowed down. One step. Then another. Then another.

Then the bedroom door opened.

\* \* \*

Lauren sat up. She was back in the present, in Bethnal Green, a student revising for her 'A' levels; not a little girl of seven lying on her mum's bed. Inside her chest there was a niggling feeling, a zig-zag line of something; fear, panic, she wasn't sure. Her neck was stiff, her mouth dry. She pushed off the covers and pulled on some clothes. She walked sluggishly downstairs and into the kitchen. Her father's letters were still on the table. They'd all been put back in their envelopes. The only one that was unfolded was the one from the solicitor. She picked it up and felt a flash of annoyance. She folded it and shoved it back into its envelope. She hesitated for a second then she walked across to the pedal bin and dropped it in.

What right did some solicitor have to ask her to come into her office and hear about her father's appeal? Surely it should be the other way round. She should be the one who was going in and *telling them* what she had seen, what she had experienced. Then, maybe they wouldn't be so keen to take his side.

After tidying the other letters back into the plastic folder she stared at the bin. Why not go up to the solicitor's and put them straight? This thought made her feel instantly better. She would go and see them. She would tell them that she wanted no further contact with Robert Slater. She plucked the letter out of the pedal bin and smoothed it out on the table.

At eight-forty she rang the solicitor's. She held her mobile tightly while it connected. She'd go to their offices and let them see her. Living proof that she had survived. Living proof of the awful thing her father did ten years ago.

'Rachel Morris speaking,' a voice said.

'Hello,' Lauren said, shakily, her resolve faltering.

'Can I help you? It's Rachel Morris here.'

'I rang because . . . I got a letter from you.'

'May I ask your name?'

'Lauren Ashe.'

'Miss Ashe. Thank you for calling. It's very good to hear from you.'

'I wanted to come in and speak with you? Today.'

'Today . . . em . . . Of course. I've got some free time later this afternoon. About two-thirty?'

It meant missing one of her classes but it was better to get it over with.

'You have the address? We're just round the corner from Holborn tube station? The central line?'

'I know how to get there,' Lauren said.

'We'll see you later, then. I'll look forward to it!'

Lauren cut the call irritated by the woman's voice, full of light and gaiety. She could have been making a hairdresser's appointment. Maybe her mood would change when Lauren told her what she remembered. Then she might not be so bright and breezy.

# 13

Holborn was even busier than where she lived. She stepped out of the tube station and felt the flow of people pulling her in one direction. She stood back by the edge of the pavement looking at the map in front of her. The street she needed was across the way and she pushed through the throng of people and waited by the crossing. When the lights turned red the cars were still blocking the crossing and she and many others had to thread their way through.

The door to the solicitor's had an entry bell and she pressed it and spoke her name into an intercom. When she walked in the receptionist told her to take a seat. It seemed only a second later when a woman burst out of a door.

'Miss Ashe,' she said, holding her hand out.

Lauren stood up. The woman moved towards her and she felt she had no option but to take her hand and shake it.

'I'm Rachel Morris. For my sins!' she said in a jolly way.

Lauren followed her into the room. She was a big lady and was wearing a black jacket and trousers over a white shirt. On the lapel of her jacket was what looked like a pink knitted brooch in the shape of a flower. Rachel Morris noticed her looking and began to pull at the petals.

'My mum knitted this. I happened to say I'd seen one and liked it and she made it for me. Several of my friends have liked it and she's done some for them. She hasn't stopped knitting for the last couple of months!'

Lauren nodded, not knowing what to say.

'What am I going on about! Do sit down. Can I get you tea or coffee? Or water?' she asked.

Lauren shook her head. The phone beeped lightly as though it didn't really want to interrupt anything.

'Excuse me,' Rachel Morris said.

Lauren looked around the office while the solicitor was speaking on the phone. Her eyes were moving here and there, eventually settling on the frosted window which seemed to have several holiday postcards stuck to it. All the while she was forcing herself to focus, to think about why she was there. It wasn't for small talk or pleasantries. It was to tell this woman, in no uncertain terms, that she wanted nothing to do with her father. She didn't want to receive letters from him, or know about his appeal. She didn't care what he did and if this solicitor wanted to know why she would describe what she'd seen on that day when her mother and sister were murdered.

Rachel Morris was trying to catch her eye. Lauren looked at her. She put her hand over the mouthpiece of the receiver and mouthed the word *Sorry*.

She'd almost decided not to come at all. That

lunchtime she'd had a call from Jessica in St Agnes. *What are you doing?* Jessica had said and she'd said, *Just the usual! College.* She had lied. She had covered up this trip because she knew it would send her aunt into a frenzy of worry. On the way out of the house she realised she'd forgotten the letter with the address and had to go back to get it.

'Sorry about that,' Rachel Morris said.

Lauren looked at her. She'd been too absorbed in her own thoughts to notice that the phone call had ended. The receiver was hooked back onto the set and Rachel Morris was sitting up straight with her elbows on the desk looking expectantly at her. Lauren cleared her throat.

'I would like you to ask my father . . .'

Rachel Morris pulled a pad from a pile of papers, picked up a pen, and sat waiting for Lauren to finish. Lauren made a small cough.

'I don't wish to receive letters from my father any more. I would like you to tell him.'

Rachel Morris's expression did not change. Her head moved as if she were about to nod in agreement. She waited. Lauren felt she had to go on speaking.

'I don't like getting letters from him. I have no interest in him and I would rather he left me alone.'

Rachel Morris wrote a couple of things down and looked back at Lauren. Her face was full of sympathy. She still did not speak.

'I'm all right now. I go to college. I have friends. I have my family.'

'Your aunt and uncle?' Rachel Morris said, gently.

She nodded. What was the point in telling her that Donny had gone? It was none of her business. In any case she had started writing again. Lauren was looking at the top of her head. There was a thin line of grey along the parting of her hair. The rest of it was brown.

'So that's all I want to say,' she said, shuffling about the seat as if she was going to get up.

Rachel Morris finished what she was writing and looked up at her. It seemed as though she'd written a couple of paragraphs when Lauren had only said one thing.

'What's that?'

'This is just so that I can report back to Mr Slater.'

'But why so much?'

'Solicitors. We go on and on about things. It's our job. Would you like to see what I've written?'

Lauren shook her head.

'Is there anything else you'd like to say?'

She waved her hand.

'May I, before you go, just tell you one or two things about Mr Slater's appeal? In case things are reported in the press that may concern you?'

'I don't want to know about him.'

'I understand but you may read things in the newspaper which—'

'I won't read it. I'll ignore it.'

'Do you ever remember a children's entertainer coming to your house?'

The question surprised her. She hadn't wanted to be drawn into a conversation. She'd said her piece and really she wanted to get up and go. Rachel Morris was waiting though. She wanted an answer to the question and Lauren could have just stood up and said *No* and been on her way but there was something that held her there. An image of a clown's face formed in her head. It wasn't the first time she'd thought of it.

'I'm not sure what you mean,' she said.

'You know, when parents organise a birthday party? They sometimes pay for entertainers? Magicians, storytellers, clowns? That sort of thing? Can you remember if your mother organised a party for you and hired an entertainer?'

'I don't know. I'm not sure. My mum didn't really like parties. I think I might have gone to one at a friend's house. I think there was a clown there.'

'How old were you?'

'I don't remember. Look, what's this got to do with anything?'

'Four years ago a man called William Doyle was arrested and charged with the murder of a mother and child at a house in Rochester. He had formed a relationship with the woman and then when it was finished he became obsessive and killed her. And the child. While in custody his DNA was taken and he was also charged with the death of a woman and her baby in Bournemouth three years before.'

'What are you saying? Is this what my father is trying to say? That someone else did it?'

'This man, William Doyle made a living as a children's

entertainer. That's how he met both of these women. A couple of other women have since come forward and said that he was a violent man.'

'My mother would never have got involved with anyone else.'

'This William Doyle was living and working in Bethnal Green ten years ago when your mother and sister were killed.'

'So, my father is trying to blame it on him?'

Rachel Morris sat impassive, her lips drawn tightly together. It looked as though her pleasant mood was crumbling.

'I saw my father. I saw him standing by my mother's body. He didn't know that I was watching because he thought he'd already killed me. *I saw him.*'

Lauren wasn't crying but her voice felt like it was scraping against metal. Her legs were clamped together, her feet pressed hard into the floor. In her hands she saw her silly Disney slides. She must have taken them out of her hair. She put them back in, faking concentration. Rachel Morris looked as though she was thinking about what she was going to say.

'I just ask one thing of you, Miss Ashe. Can you consider for one moment whether it is possible that what you thought you saw that awful day was in fact something different?'

Lauren opened her mouth to disagree but Rachel Morris put her hand up and continued.

'Could it have been that what you saw was your father

discovering the body of his wife?'

Lauren stood up. She'd been there long enough.

'He had a knife in his hand,' she said.

'Could it be that he took the knife out of your mother's wound thinking in some misguided way that it would help her?'

'He ran away. He could have called an ambulance but he ran away.'

'He thought you were all dead. He was in a state of shock.'

'I don't believe in this story and I don't wish to receive any more letters from him. I don't want any contact with him. Will you tell him that?'

'I will, Miss Ashe. Thank you so much for coming to see me.'

She turned and walked away, out of Rachel Morris's office. She didn't say a word to the receptionist, just pressed the exit button and left the building.

Now, maybe he would leave her alone.

# 14

Lauren was sipping from a glass of vodka that was thick with fruit juice and tasted like a frozen smoothie. It was the third that she'd had in less than an hour. She wasn't feeling cold, she was warm and fuzzy and relaxed. She was sitting cross-legged on the floor and there was loud music playing from her CD player which was on the coffee table. Across the room Julie and Ryan were on the sofa wrapped around each other. Julie looked ghost white against Ryan Lassiter's deep brown skin. She was wearing a shocking pink top over skinny white jeans. She was like a doll. Ryan was in his usual tightly fitting, well ironed, heavily labelled outfit. His trainers were snow white.

They were an unlikely pair and yet Ryan was stroking Julie's shoulder in an affectionate way and he was listening to all the things she was saying and laughing and teasing her.

His mate, Dexy, was on the other side of the coffee table drinking from a can of beer. He was lighter skinned than Ryan and his hair was shorter, almost shaved into his head. From time to time he pulled his mobile out of his shirt pocket and tapped out a text.

They'd arrived late, about nine.

'Dexy, this is my mate, Lauren,' Julie said, pulling Ryan ahead into the kitchen.

'Hi, Lorraine,' Dexy said looking her up and down.

'It's Lauren,' she said.

After some commotion, pouring out the drinks, putting the beers into the fridge, the vodka into the freezer, pouring the crisps and tacos into bowls, Julie pulled Lauren upstairs to get the CD player.

'What are you wearing!' Julie said, in a loud whisper.

Lauren looked down at her clothes. She was wearing clean versions of what she usually wore. Jeans and a loose shirt over a vest top.

'You don't make the best of yourself!' Julie said, tugging at the shirt until it came off. 'That's better!'

The vest top was tight fitting and Lauren didn't feel particularly comfortable, her arms bare and her tiny breasts outlined by the stretchy fabric.

'And the hair!'

Julie pulled the tie out of her hair and it fell loose. Lauren felt it on tickle her bare skin, the tops of her arms, her chest.

'That's better.'

Lauren walked into the living room with a drink in one hand and her other hand holding her hair out of her face. When she sat down she let it hang forward like a curtain. Dexy didn't seem to notice the change. He didn't seem the slightest bit interested. He sat as far away from her as he could and answered questions in a not bothered voice.

She sat on the floor and listened to music while Julie

and Ryan chatted, including her from time to time. Once they started kissing Lauren looked away, staring into the buttons and dials of the CD player, sipping the vodka. When Dexy went to the kitchen for another beer, she held her glass up for a refill. It came back stronger than before. When Julie went for a refill later Lauren held her glass up and Julie brought it back frothing over with added lemonade. It bubbled down the back of her throat.

For the first time since coming back from the solicitor's, she was feeling better. The indignation that she had felt whenever she thought about Rachel Morris's words was softening. Being completely alone in the house meant that she'd thought of nothing else. When Jessica rang, that morning, she was tempted to tell, to pour it all out to her. But Jessica was brimming over with stuff of her own. She'd got a temporary receptionist's job in a hotel and an old friend who she hadn't seen for years, who had been travelling in South America, had come back home. Lauren could hardly get a word in edgeways. *How are the cats?* she'd asked towards the end of the phone call.

The vodka was nice. It was so cold it was hurting her teeth but it made her feel soft as though all her hard edges had gone. She glanced over at Dexy. He was quite nice looking in a way. She thought for a moment of Nathan and his T-shirt that said *Cuba!* She wondered what he was doing. She pictured him sitting at his laptop in the attic room.

'Look at Lauren! She looks so serious!' Julie said, jumping up to change the CD. Faster music came on and she began dancing by herself, jumping up and down, like a puppet.

'Come on, you three!' she said.

Ryan stayed where he was, brushing at the fabric of his jeans. Dexy stared down into his mobile. Lauren got up and went out into the kitchen and got another drink. Moments later Julie followed her.

'Lauren, is it all right if Ryan and I . . .'

She pointed up to the ceiling. It took Lauren a moment to work out what she meant. Then the penny dropped. She wanted to go upstairs with Ryan. Up to a bedroom.

'Go to my aunt's old room. There's no sheets or anything but . . .'

Julie gave her a kiss on the cheek.

'It'll give you and Dexy some space,' she said.

Ryan looked apologetic and embarrassed as Julie pulled him out of the room. Lauren sat down on the sofa. She drank great gulps from her drink, her head feeling light and mildly dizzy. When she heard the bedroom door shut upstairs she sat up straight and patted the seat beside her and spoke.

'You could come and sit here,' she said, keeping her words steady.

Dexy stood up, put his phone in his pocket, patted down his trousers and stepped across to the sofa. For a moment she didn't know what to do. She felt herself slumping towards him so she tried to sit up straight. She turned to him, pulled her hair back and leant forward to kiss him. He kissed her back, pushing his tongue into her mouth. Instantly she knew she didn't want him. She pulled her face back and put her hand up to stop him coming any closer.

'Sorry,' she said.

She was tired. She wanted to lie down on the sofa and go to sleep. Dexy seemed unperturbed. He stood up.

'Never mind, Lorraine. You're not really my type any way.'

'Lauren,' she said.

'See you around.'

She was disgruntled. She shifted around on the sofa as Dexy went out of the room and walked up the hallway. It wasn't as if she even liked him. She heard the front door close. Then she lay down on the settee, stretching her legs out. She felt exhausted. She heard a laugh from upstairs. It sounded like Julie was having a good time. She closed her eyes and pushed her face into the cushion. There was more laughter, maybe from some kids out in the street. She felt drowsy and images formed in her head of laughing faces. In the middle, somewhere, the face of a clown emerged, with white skin, blood red lips and dead eyes. She mumbled and turning onto her side she shook the pictures away and in seconds sunk into a deep sleep.

When she woke up the house was pitch dark. It was late, she could tell by the quiet of the street outside the window. She tried to raise herself but felt nauseous. Where were Julie and Ryan? Were they still upstairs? She didn't have the strength to call out. In any case they were probably asleep. She let her head drop back onto the cushion and felt herself drawn back into sleep again.

Later it was light. She lifted her head and felt the same sick feeling that she had felt in the night. Her head was heavy and her skin seemed raw. She tried to sit up but then decided against it. Looking down she recognised her duvet. Julie must have covered her up.

She could hear birds singing outside. It was high pitched and in bursts, like just one line of a song then silence. She closed her eyes. She wasn't going to go back to sleep but her head felt softer in the dark. She pulled the duvet around her. The birdsong seemed further away. After a few moments Rachel Morris came into her head and she remembered the big knitted brooch. How bright and breezy the woman had been. It was as if she was telling her that she had inherited a million pounds from a distant aunt. Instead of that she was asking her questions about the past. *Do you ever remember a children's entertainer coming to your house?*

The only children's entertainer that she had ever seen was at her neighbour's daughters' tenth birthday party. The twins were older than her but she still played with them now and then. Molly was friendly with her mother and sometimes Lauren went there to give her mother a break. *Mum needs some time with baby Daisy*, Molly would say, taking her hand warmly and marching her back to the next house but one where she spent a morning or an afternoon with the twins.

The birthday party was after school one Friday. Her mum had bought her new clothes, a Disney T-shirt and jeans that had sequins sewn into them. Possibly it was around the time her mother and sister were killed. Was it a month before? A week before? The previous day? Time was difficult to measure from where she was. There was Before and there was After. Everything Before seemed to happen at the same time, all on the same page. Afterwards time stretched out like the chapters of a book.

The children's entertainer was a clown who did magic tricks. He stood pulling scarves from one of his sleeves. Lots of scarves tied together, one after the other, the colours of a rainbow. Then he scrunched them all up and fed them into his mouth and appeared to chew for a long time then take a great swallow. The scarves were gone. It looked as though he had eaten them all.

He was tall. His face was long and thin and his ears stuck out. He had thick make-up on and his lips were drawn down at the side so that he looked sad. He wore red trousers with yellow dots. Over the top was a purple jacket that had long tails at the back. He wanted several volunteers she remembered and the twins seemed to get picked every time. Once he pointed at her and she felt a twist of panic inside but he was only making a joke about something. His hair was red and curly. He seemed jolly but Lauren hadn't enjoyed his smile or his tricks. She'd found him a bit of a worry and kept thinking about the rainbow coloured scarves sitting in his stomach.

Her mum had arrived with Daisy while he was still

doing tricks and she'd watched him for a while.

When the party was over Lauren sat on the arm of a chair by the bay window and waited for her mum to finish talking to Molly. She heard Molly sing out a *Goodbye, thanks again,* and the front door closed. A bald man in ordinary clothes walked away from the house. He was carrying a big bag and as he opened the gate to leave he turned back to the house and she saw that it was the clown. He had no make-up on and the wig was gone but his ears stuck out and his face was long. She knew it was him because his mouth was turned down at the sides.

Was this the man that Rachel Morris had talked about?

Lauren opened her eyes and saw that the light was brighter. The sun was reaching in through the gap in the curtains. She lifted her head and looked around the room. There were glasses and beer cans scattered across the floor. She sat up, her palm across her stomach as if to control the nausea she felt. She got slowly to her feet and walked out of the room. She called *Julie* up the stairs and listened. She called again, louder but there was no answer.

She was on her own. Julie and Ryan had gone. A bubble of self pity welled up inside her. Jessica and Donny had gone. She had no one. As well as feeling sick with a hangover she was going to cry. She forced herself to walk up the stairs to her room. She went straight in closing the door behind her. There was no duvet on the bed. She remembered it was downstairs. She sat down on the mattress and then lay back.

She thought of the children's entertainer. When he left the twins' house he'd looked ordinary like any other man who might walk up the street. He'd put the clown into the big bag he'd been carrying. She'd imagined it fully formed like a life-sized puppet that had been folded in half and zipped away. In her head its eyes were blinking at the darkness of the bag its cherry red lips pulled tight and gasping for air as if it was suffocating.

Rachel Morris would want to know about this man.

# 15

The sound of her ring tone roused Lauren just after ten. It was coming from downstairs in the living room. She moved quickly but missed the call. The name *Julie* was on the screen. Moments later the beep of a message came. *Hope you're not feeling too bad. See you at college. Then I'll tell all about Ryan!!!*

She went into the kitchen and got a large glass of water. She drank it down and then went back up to her room. The pink plastic envelope caught her eye. It was lying crooked on the edge of her chest of drawers. She had an urge to go and right it, to line up right angle against right angle. She reached her hand out as if to do it but as her fingers touched the cold plastic she picked it up and took it across to her bed. After a few moments of indecision she sat down and tipped the contents out. Reaching across to her bedside table she picked up an elastic hairband and pulled her hair back into it. Then she ruffled through the pages and empty envelopes until she found the ones she wanted.

Two letters had been written on a computer. The longer one had been sent to her two years before. She held them in her hand and felt a stirring of emotion. A mixture of trepidation and an ache of loss. Her father, Robert Slater, had dropped out of her life ten years ago. And yet, in her mind, there were some pictures of him forming, images unfolding, memories from Before, when she was very young.

He was there in Somers Park at the end of Hazelwood Road. He was standing by the swing. She must have been in the swing because she remembered coming towards him and moving away. She reached out to touch him, her hand stretched as far as it would go and when she got almost to the point of contact the swing dropped back and took her away. He was slightly turned away from her, his mobile phone at his ear, one hand in mid air waiting for the swing to get close enough to give it a push. Then he was there facing her and she was climbing out of the swing. He hoisted her up on his shoulder and she saw a small pen behind his ear. Just sitting there. A pen. *Daddy, I can see a pen,* she must have said because the next minute she was sitting on a low brick wall with the pen in her hand. *The man in the betting shop gives them to me,* he said.

He was in the shed at the bottom of the garden. He was standing at a high bench smoking a cigarette. *Can I help, Daddy?* she must have said because then she was sitting on grass with some small brown plastic pots. There was a bag of earth by the side of her; it was her job to put earth in each of the pots. Then he came out and squatted down beside her with a packet of seeds. She took them, tiny and hard, and poked them into the damp earth. *Now*

*they go into the shed for a few weeks and then when they start to grow
we plant them in the ground.*

In the kitchen. She was sitting at the table. There was
no baby so maybe it was before Daisy came. There was a
plate in front of her with chicken and rice and gravy. In
among the rice were peas. *I don't like peas, Daddy.* How
could he have forgotten? He'd tutted, his face red from
the heat of the stove. He sat down beside her and with a
fork picked each pea out of the rice. The door opened,
she thought, and her mother came in. *Look at this! I
accidentally put peas in Lolly's meal.*

*Lolly.* Her father had called her by her nickname. She
hadn't remembered that until this moment. She sat back
on the bed, the paper of the other letters crinkling as she
moved. In the hand was a typed letter that she should
have received when she fifteen.

*Dear Lauren, I haven't written for a while because I've been a bit
down. My asthma got worse and they couldn't find the right
antibiotics so I've been ill. On the bright side though I'm typing this
on a computer. This is because I've just done a course on IT in the
education wing. While you are swotting for your GCSEs I am using
two fingers to type and feeling pleased with myself if I can 'save' a
document. You'll probably laugh at that. All you kids know
everything there is to know about computers. It's us 'oldies' that have
the problem.*

*I miss you. Every day I think of you and wonder what you look
like, what sort of clothes you buy, what sort of music you like. I
imagine that you're quite tall and probably thin like your mother*

*was. I think you would have long brown hair and you would be pretty, like your mother was.*

*I probably shouldn't write about your mother but part of me thinks you're not going to read this letter anyway so I'll go on. When your mother and I got married we were very happy for a few years. You mustn't believe the stuff that came out in the newspapers about me having lots of affairs. It's not true. Your mother and me made a good couple, for a few years. But your mother was a person who always looked on the dark side of life. She worried and worried about everything. When you were little she tried to protect you from everything. It wore her down, it changed her into a very defensive person. We grew apart and yes, I did leave for a while, but I came back and tried to make a go of it. Then I met Georgia. I was building a conservatory for her and we became close. I tried to tell your mother but she didn't want to know. She wanted us to go on as we were.*

*I didn't kill your mother or Daisy but I can see why I was a good suspect. And then of course, the things that you said at the trial. That confirmed it. I don't blame you for that. You told the truth, you said what you thought you saw. Maybe one day you will realise that you only saw part of the picture. I don't know. Whatever happens, even if the truth is never revealed I won't blame you. I will love you until the day I die.*

*DadXXXXXXXXXX*

Lauren picked up the second letter. It had been sent to her about a year before. She would have been sixteen. She didn't read it all, just the last paragraph.

*My solicitor has told me that some new evidence has come to light and it looks as though we might be able to get a second appeal. I won't go into details now but I'm keeping my fingers crossed. Maybe one day, in the not too distant future, they will say that I have been wrongly convicted. And on that day you and I will meet again.*

*Much, much love, DadXXXXXXXX*

She put it down, on the bed. Without moving too much she lifted her legs up and lay on her side, her head on the pillow. She felt confused. The certainties she had in her head seemed muddy, not so clear. If only there was someone she could talk to, Jessica maybe. But Jessica had never liked to talk about that time. And the truth was that Lauren had hardly ever asked anything about it. For the first couple of years she had gone to see a counsellor, Mrs Paxton, at St Michael's Hospital. Once a month she had visited her in a blue room that had a giant tree outside its window. Mrs Paxton talked with her in a gentle voice. She wore cardigans even when it was very hot and nodded a lot as though she agreed with every single thing that Lauren uttered. She always wore a badge that had her name on it, *Jenny*, but Lauren had never called her that. When there was a quiet moment she looked out of the window at the tree. Some days it seemed full of birds, other days the branches were empty. As if the birds had heard about a better tree somewhere else. A couple of times she saw a squirrel running crazily up the trunk and one day some men came with a buzzing saw and trimmed the branches. Mrs Paxton kept looking round and tutting at the noise.

Jessica never asked about these sessions. If Lauren mentioned anything she said, *That's good* or *I expect so*. At seven and eight the conversation about what had happened to Lauren's mother and baby sister was not something Jessica or Donny wanted to have. It only ever came about by accident. The murder of her mother and sister. Her father in prison. These things were like jagged rocks and most of the time Lauren, Jessica and Danny navigated their way around them. Occasionally something forced them onto the subject.

'Why didn't Daddy live with Mum and me and Daisy?'

'Where did Daddy live?'

'Why was Daddy so angry with Mum?'

Mrs Paxton gave her vague and smiley answers to these things. Jessica did not even try. She became red faced, her mouth tightly shut as though her answers were too hot and her words, if they came out, might set fire to the room. Donny just looked confused. *It's hard to explain what people do, Lolly. Sometimes there's just no answers.* So Lauren steered clear. One day she said she didn't want to go and see Mrs Paxton any more. Jessica seemed relieved and she took her to the cinema in Perranporth instead.

Now she stood up and looked out of her bedroom window at the back gardens below. It was almost eleven but it was still quiet. Sunday stretched ahead of her long and empty. She had plenty of work to do but it all seemed suddenly unimportant. The exams, the grades, the projects, the references for uni. All of it was worth nothing against this heavy thing she had hanging over her. Her father, who had been blamed for everything, was still fighting back, protesting his innocence.

If she could talk to someone. If she could just be with someone.

If she wasn't so *alone*.

She picked up her mobile. She scrolled down her contacts list. She skipped past Donny and Jessica. Most of the rest were in Cornwall, old friends that she thought she'd left behind for good. There were a couple of new names, kids from her classes but no one she honestly wanted to ring. Julie was the only person she knew well but she had no urge to ring her.

She saw the name *Nathan*.

It made her stop. It was over a week since she'd seen him outside the college. She could ring him. She could even *tell* him what had been happening. He knew all her secrets. She held her mobile up to her chin wondering what to do. How well did she know him? Could she really trust him? She'd only been in his company for a few hours at most.

She reached round to the back of her neck and felt her hair tied tightly. She couldn't help but smile to herself. *A mermaid.*

She pressed the call button.

'Yep.'

'Nathan?' she said.

'That's me.'

'It's . . . it's Lauren.'

'Lauren,' he said, his voice softening. 'It's good to hear from you. I didn't think you'd ring!'

'I've been busy.

'I thought you'd dumped me!'

'Don't be silly. How could I? We're not together . . .'

'Now, you're dumping me!'

'No,' she said, half exasperated, feeling her face break into a silly smile, 'Why don't you come round to my place?'

'Oh . . .'

There was silence and she heard a sigh. Was he turning her down?

'I'd love to but I'm decorating. I'm halfway through a room. I could come later? Tonight?'

'I could help,' she said, 'I'm good with paintbrushes.'

'But . . . don't you mind about the house?'

'I've been there before, remember.'

'If you're sure . . .'

She ended the call.

Hazelwood Road. It pulled her back time and time again.

# 16

Lauren and Nathan finished painting the dining room about three. After they cleaned up Nathan said he had to take the dogs to the park. Lauren thought he meant a walk to Somers Park but he picked up his car keys from the hall table.

'I must look a sight,' she said, looking down to see paint stains on her top and jeans.

'Not to me, you don't,' he said.

Nathan had no problem stating his feelings. Lauren found it disconcerting. She avoided his gaze and made a point of brushing at her clothes, using her thumb nail to try and scrape off some dried paint. The dogs were making yelping noises and turning in circles and she followed Nathan as he led them out to his car that was parked half up on the pavement. She felt a spring in her step. Her hangover was gone but more than that she felt pleased to be with Nathan. Even being in the house hadn't upset her. She'd stayed downstairs and concentrated on the bit of the wall she'd been painting. Most of the time, with Nathan's chatter in the back of her head, she'd forgotten where she was.

He never mentioned her past. It was as if he hadn't

found out about it at all. She was grateful for that.

Nathan put the dogs in the back of the car and Lauren got into the passenger seat. The engine started and loud music filled the car. Lauren looked round to see that Prince and Duke were sitting patiently. They drove off and Nathan began to sing along with the song that was playing. They didn't talk for most of the journey, Nathan pushing the buttons of the radio, changing channels every time a track came on that he didn't like. She didn't mind the lack of conversation. It was relaxing. It was easy.

'Where are we going?' she said, in a gap between songs.

'Wanstead Park. Do you know it?'

She shook her head.

'Big green space. It's good. The dogs get a long run.'

Wanstead Park had numbers of people on it but it was so big that they hardly ever came close to anyone. The dogs ran forward and then came back. They shot off at angles and sometimes one chased the other until they started a play fight. When other dogs were on the horizon they stood still, tense, waiting to see if there was a threat. When there wasn't they gambolled about playing as thought they had met long lost friends.

Nathan told her where his parents were.

'In France for two weeks. Driving round. Staying here and there. I'm the official dog walker/house-painter/gardener/telephone answering service while they're away.'

'I'm on my own as well,' she said.

'How come?' he said.

She explained about Jessica and Donny and their break up. The whole story came out in a paragraph, an abbreviated version that left out the grief and upset.

'Jessica's like, your mother's sister?'

Lauren nodded. The mention of her mother made her stiffen. Was he going to start talking about it? If he did, if he started asking her stuff, details, she wasn't sure she'd be able to answer.

'So if your aunt has gone back to Cornwall does that mean you'll go back as well?'

She nodded, relieved that he didn't seem to want to pry.

Nathan threw a ball so that the dogs would run after it.

When she went back to Cornwall it would mean she probably wouldn't see Nathan again, or Julie Bell or any of the other kids that she'd come into contact with over the past few months. Nathan walked on a few metres. She felt her good mood slipping away. She wanted to go back to Cornwall and yet *some* good things had happened in London. Nathan stopped and picked up the ball from the ground where Prince had left it. He threw it high so that it arced into the sky and went far across the grass. Prince and Duke tore after it. He turned and smiled at her. The sun was in his eyes and he held one hand over them to block it out. He looked so natural, so easy.

'I won't be going back for a couple of weeks,' she said, positively, 'until my last exam is over.'

'Doesn't bother me,' he said, when she drew level with him. 'You go back to Cornwall.'

She didn't answer, puzzled at his apparent disinterest

'In September I go down to Exeter Uni. Play your cards right and I'll come and see you.'

'You're kidding,' she said.

He shook his head and threw one of his arms around her shoulder.

'You're not getting rid of me that easily.'

Back at the house Lauren watched the dogs eating. They were standing in the glossy kitchen. On the draining board were the paint brushes they'd washed earlier, small splashes of white paint spattered on the tiles behind the sink. Lauren picked up a cloth and wiped them off.

The dogs had their noses in bowls and there was the sound of slurping and crunching.

'That's nothing,' Nathan said. 'You should hear me eating.'

'I have to go,' she said, smiling. 'I've the rest of my revision to do.'

'Stay round here,' he said.

'I can't. You know I can't.'

He looked momentarily uneasy and she wondered whether he was going to start talking about it now. She'd been anxious all afternoon waiting for him to ask questions. *What was it like? What did it feel like to have someone try to kill you?*

'You wouldn't feel comfortable here. I understand. I tell

you what though. You could sleep in the living room on the sofa-bed. I won't come near. I'll be in up in my room and I don't sleepwalk . . .'

She shook her head.

'I've got all my revision stuff at home. And my exam starts at nine.'

'You're on your own. I'm on my own. It would be really good to have you here. You could stay on the ground floor. Everything you need is down here. Shower room, toilet, kitchen. You don't have to go upstairs for anything.'

'I couldn't,' she said.

'My parents are away until Wednesday week. Ten days of peace.'

'Why don't you come and stay at my house?' she said, 'There's a spare bedroom.'

'I can't leave the dogs.'

'Oh.'

'Here,' he said, picking up the car keys from the hall table, 'let me give you a lift.'

'No, I feel like a walk. Really. I'll call you,' she said, pausing at the front door.

'Oh no,' he said. 'The *I'll call you* line again.'

'I'll call you tomorrow, after the exam. I promise.'

She leant across and gave him a kiss on the cheek.

It was past six when she got home. She opened the door and stepped into the stuffy quiet of the house. It was hot, the air felt thick. She took her jacket off and hung it on the empty hallstand. She walked through into the kitchen and pushed open the window over the sink. Fresher air came in, so did the noises from the nearby gardens, children shouting, a hint of music from somewhere, the buzz of a lawn mower. Turning away she saw the empty vodka bottle on the floor by the bin. She thought of Julie and Ryan and his friend Dexy from the night before. What had she been thinking of? Was she so desperate for company that she would get herself drunk and offer herself up to some kid she'd only just met and didn't even like?

She went upstairs and sorted out the work she needed to look through for the next day's exam. By the side of her bed was the pink enevelope filled again with her father's letters. She picked it up and put it in her drawer, underneath her clothes. She'd spent enough time taking the letters out and putting them back. Now they were packed away for good.

She sat back on her bed reading through her revision notes. A short while later she heard a sound, like a knock coming from the direction of the front door. It was unusual. Like someone was using the letterbox rather than the bell. She got up and walked onto the landing. Looking down she saw, on the hall mat, a white envelope. Her shoulders dropped as she plodded down the stairs and picked it up. Her name was on the front in neat handwriting, *Miss Lauren Ashe*. She opened it. Inside was a short handwritten note and a business card from *Barrat and Morris Solicitors*.

*Dear Miss Ashe, It was so nice to meet you on Friday. I do hope you were not too upset by our conversation. I just wanted you to know that you can contact me any time for a chat. Yours Rachel Morris.*

*P.S. I was really interested when you said saw a children's entertainer at a friend's party. If you felt you could give me any more information on this I would be very grateful.*

On the card was an email address and two printed numbers, the Holborn office and a mobile. Underneath, handwritten, was a home number.

Irritated, she opened the front door and looked out onto the street. There was no sign of anyone walking by or any car just moving off. She went back in and chucked the note on the hall table. Hadn't she made herself completely clear? Why couldn't they just leave her alone? It wasn't enough that she was receiving letters by post now it was by hand.

She simply didn't want to have to think about the clown any more. The man meant nothing to her, he was just someone she'd seen once at a party doing tricks and making kids laugh. Afterwards, she'd seen him leaving Molly's house. That was the sum total of what she remembered.

Or was it?

Something else was there, in the back of her mind, some niggling thing that was associated with the clown. She tried to concentrate but nothing emerged. The memory was there but she couldn't quite grasp it. It came tantalisingly close, coming up from deep water only to turn at the last minute and disappear again.

She picked up the card. She should ring this woman.

Tell her once again to leave her alone. She could complain to somebody. Harassment. The solicitor had no right to come to her actual home. She looked crossly at the card. In the middle of the print was a drawing of a set of scales. A picture representing what the firm stood for. Justice.

She patted her pockets looking for her phone. But even as she was doing it something else was coming into her head. Another card that she had held, another picture, a name and phone number. A fragment of something. Hadn't she just been thinking about the past? About the clown. And then, as if a page in a magazine had been turned it was all there laid out in her head, crystal clear.

A yellow business card that had the face of a clown on it. A hand-drawn picture that took up most of the space on the card. Only the red lips were coloured in. Along the bottom was some print. It was the name of the children's entertainer but she couldn't remember that because she hadn't bothered to read the words. She'd been too busy looking at the picture and then at the man who had given it to her mum.

It was a visit to Woolworth's. Her mum was going to buy her a present. For being good. For playing with Daisy. Her mum was wheeling the pushchair but had stopped to talk to someone she knew. Lauren ran ahead to the toy aisle.

*Don't go too far, Lauren*, her mum called.

Lauren was looking along the shelves. Her eye scanned what was there. There was a line of soft toys. Rabbits, dogs and monkeys. They all hung from little hooks on the rack. She loved the monkey immediately. She picked it off and ran her fingers over its dark silky fur. She held it to her chest as if it was already hers. Then she became aware of an adult standing next to her, a man.

*It's very cuddly*, he said, looking at the monkey.

She was surprised. He was speaking to her.

*Yes*, she said, politely.

*I've got a rabbit behind my back. I wonder if you can guess which hand it's in.*

She looked at the man more carefully. His ears stuck out and his face was long.

*Which hand?* he said with a half-smile.

She pointed at one side and he brought the rabbit out with a flourish. From behind she could hear her name being called and she sensed the pushchair coming closer.

*What's that, Lauren?* her mum said, looking questioningly at the man.

*Hello!* he said, replacing the rabbit on its hook. *Weren't you both at the party in Hazelwood Road. Last week?*

Her mum nodded.

*I was the children's entertainer. The clown.*

*Oh, yes, of course. I didn't recognise you. Of course.*

Her mum and the clown started to talk but Lauren didn't take much notice. She picked up the rabbit and looked at it for a moment. It was a grey colour and its fur was very soft. She hesitated and looked sideways at the clown. He was saying something about Daisy and laughing. Then he took a card out of a pocket and gave it to her mum.

*You might decide to have a party. You can get me on my mobile most of the time*, he said.

He took a couple of steps away from the toys and walked off quickly, as if he had somewhere he had to be. Lauren wondered whether he'd forgotten the rabbit that he was going to buy. She put it back and picked up the monkey again. Her mum was holding the card.

*Can I have a look?* she said.

Her mum gave her the card. There was a drawing of a clown's face. The red lips were smiling. It didn't look anything like the clown she had seen in the twins' house.

*Come on, let's go and pay for this*, her mum said.

*I know what I'm going to call him*, Lauren said.

*Come on. Daisy'll need feeding soon.*

*I'm going to call him Charlie. Charlie the Chimp*, she said, handing the soft toy to her mum.

While they were queuing to pay she looked out of the shop window. She saw the clown, at a bus stop, waiting behind two girls who looked a bit older than her. A bus arrived and blocked out her view. When it left, a few moments later, the girls had gone but the clown was still standing there. Then he looked at his watch and walked off up the road.

*Here you are!* her mum said, giving her the present.

She took the monkey out of its bag and held it to her chest.

\* \* \*

Lauren was surprised by the memory. She hadn't only seen the clown once. She'd seen him again. Her mum had taken his card. Had she called him? Trying to arrange Lauren's birthday party? She stood up abruptly. This was stupid. This was listening to the solicitor and the story that her father was using to clear his name. It didn't matter that her mum had met this man. It didn't matter that this clown's face was in her head now. Lauren *knew* what she'd seen that day ten years before. Her father had killed her mother and her baby sister. He had tried to kill her.

What did it matter if the clown had been there in Woolworth's?

She'd seen him again though, after that, on her doorstep. She'd opened the door and he was standing there. He didn't have any make-up on or a costume and he was poised in an odd way with both his hands behind his back.

*I've got something nice in my hand. Guess which one it's in.*

Her mum was standing behind her and didn't seem put out by what he was saying.

*Go on, guess. If you get it right you can have it to keep.*

She pointed to one side and he brought his closed hand round and held it in front of her. Then he opened the hand and Lauren saw a large glass marble. It was shot through with silver and looked rich like some jewel that might be found in a treasure chest.

*Thanks!* she said, as the clown walked past her up the hallway.

*You found us then*, her mother said, leading him down to the kitchen.

*I was just doing a party in the next road. I thought I'd pop round and talk about what you'd like me to do.*

Her mum was thinking of having a party.

The memory of it made her feel a little sick.

She went back upstairs but couldn't settle. She walked up and down the landing. How was she ever going to be calm enough to do her revision, to think about the exam the next day? How could she do that while all this other stuff was going on in her head?

She should ring the solicitor. Tell her about the clown. But how could she? How could she be drawn into this? She wanted no part of it. She wanted the past left behind, like some island that she didn't live on any more. A far away place. Maybe the solicitor wouldn't accept that though. Maybe she would keep on trying. Perhaps next time there wouldn't be a letter just a knock at the door and she would open it to find her standing there, bearing down on her, wanting to talk to her, to question her, to demand information from her.

She couldn't stay in the house any more.

She picked up her mobile and scrolled until she came to Nathan's number. Thirty minutes later he was outside in the car. She put her two bags in the back and got into the passenger seat, settling her feet amid the litter that was still there.

'Glad you changed your mind about staying,' he said.

She wasn't a fool. She knew she was trying to escape

the past by hiding in Hazelwood Road. But who would think of looking for her there?

## 17

They got back to the house before nine.

Lauren carried a couple of bags into the living room and dropped them on the floor. Nathan followed in with her other bags.

'I'll make this up,' he said, pointing to the sofa-bed.

'Thanks.'

She looked round the room. Its walls had been recently re-plastered and were salmon pink. There was just the sofa and a television in the room. That was all. It was bare. It looked completely different to what it had been when she lived there.

She'd seen the rest of the ground floor that afternoon. It had changed beyond recognition. The living room that she remembered had reached from the front to the back of the house as if a wall between two rooms had been knocked down at some point. Now the wall had been rebuilt and the living room was small and square. The other half of the big room was now a dining room its walls painted Cornflower Blue that very afternoon. The kitchen had been extended and jutted out into the garden which was still overgrown and unkempt. Under the stairs, where cupboards had been, a cloakroom had been constructed. The door opened to brilliant white tiles, a toilet and shower and washbasin. The hallway itself was still dusty and undecorated but the rest of the ground floor was like being in a new house.

Still she felt a bit strange standing there. It wasn't just a visit. She intended to stay, to *sleep* there.

The dogs were running round her. She felt her hand being nibbled.

'Let's get a pizza,' Nathan said, looking a bit awkward.

'All right.'

She was hungry. Thirty minutes later they were sitting at the kitchen table eating slices of pizza. The back doors were open and there was still enough light to see out into the garden. The dogs were sitting by their feet following the movement of the pizza slices with their eyes.

'Do you want to get a shower after this and I'll sort the bed out?' Nathan said.

She nodded. He hadn't said much to her since he picked her up. What he had said had been small talk, about the traffic or the dogs. He hadn't asked her why she had changed her mind about staying. In a way she was grateful although part of her wished she could explain, wished that she could feel easy about talking about it all with another person.

After her shower she went into the living room. She'd used the shower cap so it was only her hairline that was damp. The rest was dry and was hanging loose. The sofa bed was out and made up. The window shutters had been closed over. The television news channel was on, the sound low. She got into the sofa-bed and lay still, feeling odd. Nathan came in and sat on the bed. She felt, for a moment, as if she was a patient in a hospital bed and he was a visitor.

'You going to be all right here?' he said.

She went to say something but couldn't. The whole day weighed down on her. The hangover, the note from the solicitor, the clown that kept tumbling into her thoughts.

'It's going to be too weird for you, isn't it? Sleeping here. I'll take you home if you want. You just have to say. You could come round in the daytime for a while, get used to the place. Not that you need to get used to it, you did used to live here . . . You know . . .'

He was looking straight at her. He was worried she could tell. He was biting his lip. She had an overwhelming desire to reach out and touch him. She put her hand out and rubbed his arm. *Thank you for worrying about me*, she wanted to say.

'Now you really do look like a mermaid,' he said, his voice husky, his fingers touching the hair on her shoulders.

'You know what they say about mermaids?' she said.

'Mortals should avoid them.'

He leaned across and kissed her mouth. He pushed his hands into her hair and held it back off her face. She felt his lips brushing side to side, his fingers combing through her hair. She put her arms around his neck and he moved his body closer to her. Her chest was aching, her skin humming. She felt herself lying back and pulled him with her so that he was half on top of her. The duvet was wrinkled up between them. He went to move it away but it was caught underneath her. He tried again but it wouldn't budge. She started to giggle.

'Great!' he said, looking flushed. 'You're laughing at me!'

'I'm not,' she said but he was smiling too.

He lay on top of the duvet and put his face into her neck and she felt his mouth on her skin. His hand was resting lightly on her chest. She closed her eyes and felt her head swimming.

Then he sat up and moved back away from her.

'There's something you need to know. Seeing as I know about your ... stuff ...' he said. 'Not that my *stuff* is serious, you know like yours.'

She sat up. She hooked her hair behind her ears. He was serious all of a sudden.

'I had this long term girlfriend. Mandy. She used to live where we used to live. We started hanging out together when we were fourteen. Like boyfriend and girlfriend? We went to the same school together. We were in the same classes. Everyone knew that we were ...'

'Together?'

'Yeah. She was going to go to Exeter? The same uni as me. We were going to get a flat and stuff. And then, a few weeks before uni started she changed her mind. She said we needed some space. So she took a year out, and then went to Durham.'

'Oh,' Lauren said, pulling the duvet up around her chest.

'I think she'd decided a long while before but never said anything. I gave her this stupid ultimatum. Come to Exeter or we're finished and guess what? We finished.'

He was quiet for a moment.

'But you didn't go to uni?'

'I deferred for a year too. My parents arranged for me to go and stay with a family friend in Australia and I travelled to other places as well. They were planning to move house anyway so when I got back I wasn't living in the same place as Mandy.'

She couldn't think of anything to say.

'I don't know why I'm telling you really except that, well, she looked a bit like you. She had long hair. Like yours.'

'Like mine?'

'But . . . don't think you're a . . .'

'That I'm a substitute?' Lauren said, not quite sure where the conversation was going.

'And maybe that *was* what I first noticed about you. The hair, I mean. But you are so different to Mandy. She was always looking in the mirror, getting dressed up, putting make-up on.'

'And I'm a bit of a slob,' she said.

'No! But you don't seem to care so much about that stuff and I like that about you. You are totally unlike Mandy.'

'I do have a tragic past. That makes me unique,' she said dryly.

She tensed, wondering if he was going to ask her about

it now. *What did it feel like to have someone try to kill you?* He didn't speak though. He looked embarrassed, sorry that the subject had come up. She felt a rush of gratitude. She put out her arm and pulled him back towards her. She kissed him on the mouth and he lay beside her. She felt sleepy and let herself move down the bed a bit.

'I just thought you should know. About the hair,' he whispered.

'OK,' she yawned, 'But now I do need to sleep,' she said, 'I've got an Art exam tomorrow.'

'Why don't I sleep down here with you?'

'I don't think . . .' she said, momentarily moving back away from him.

'I mean *sleep*. Not anything else. I just thought you might feel better sleeping with someone. You know, for comfort, like mates?'

'Mates?' she laughed, 'After all this kissing?'

'No, really. All that stuff we can do during the day time. At night, we just sleep.'

'All right,' she said.

Why not? Being alone in the room might upset her. Once the lights were off and the house was quiet she might start thinking about it. The clown, the solicitor's, the day she woke up in her mum's bedroom.

'All right. We can sleep here, together. That would be good.'

'Hold that thought,' he said. 'I'll get my stuff.'

He went out of the room and she heard him up going up the stairs. She lay down, moving to one side of the sofa-bed. She put her head on the pillow. She felt tired, her eyelids heavy. Footsteps sounded from above her and she heard him coming down. He was wearing striped pyjama bottoms and a T-shirt.

'My dad's,' he explained, 'protective gear. I don't know if I can trust you.'

He got in beside her. She gave a sleepy smile.

'Turn around,' she said. 'Away from me.'

'OK,' he said, turning his back on her.

She put her arm across his waist and tucked her legs in behind his.

'In spoons,' she said, her voice husky with tiredness.

He grabbed hold of her hand and pulled her close.

# Part Three

# House of Revelations

# 18

The Art exam took place over two days. Her back was aching and so was her neck. She spent over eight hours in the Art room. There were ten kids working there with her. Julie Bell was a few benches away. She was all in black for some reason, her hair pulled back from her face by a cotton scarf. She had deep red lipstick on and heavy false eyelashes. Lauren's hair was tied back except for a thick strand from behind her ear which she pulled round her neck to fiddle with while she was working.

While she developed her piece she noticed a radio playing in the distance, some kind of jazz music that she didn't know. From time to time the buzzer went for classes and for a while the corridor outside the Art room was filled with noise, then it lessened and it was quiet again, the sound of the saxophone rising from the radio, making her stop and listen for a moment. Mostly she concentrated on her work and from time to time noticed Julie out of the corner of her eye. Julie's face was rapt, her eyelashes casting a shadow under her eyes.

When she finished, on the second day, she sat back and looked at her work. The prep was there to be seen, line drawings of dolls and houses and explorative pastels of faces through windows. One of the final collages was small, miniature, the window of a doll's house, through which it was possible to see the figures inside. The other piece was taken from the inside of the doll's house. A face looking out of a window. Across the window was barbed wire. It was a black-and-white drawing.

Her teacher had been pleased.

When she left the room Julie was waiting for her.

'Fancy coming round mine tonight?' she said. 'For a celebration.'

'I can't,' she said, turning away, working towards the exit.

'You're seeing that lad from the museum,' Julie said. 'Tell me everything.'

'I can't. I've got to go. I'm expecting a call from my aunt in Cornwall. I'll talk to you tomorrow.'

'Is your aunt called *Nathan* by any chance?' Julie shouted after her.

For the rest of the week she went to college for last-minute classes and in the house she revised. There was lots of paperwork she had to do as well as finishing the syllabuses. She didn't want to go back to her old school in St Agnes so she had to enrol at the FE college in Perranporth. She had to arrange for her teachers to forward her results and her coursework. She had to sign off from the college. It seemed that everyone had to sign her forms before she could be released.

It took her mind off her other troubles. She hardly

thought about her father or the solicitor. Even the house and its associations had faded into the background for her. Only occasionally did her eye flicker up the stairs. Mostly she kept her head down and headed for the shiny, modern kitchen. She ate at the big table. She showered in the cloakroom. She slept with Nathan on the sofa bed in the living room.

At lunchtime Nathan went to work at the museum café. The rest of the day he did jobs in the house. He painted, stripped off wallpaper and sanded the wood of window frames and doors. Morning and night he took the dogs out.

They went shopping at the supermarket, piling the food on the back seat of the car. She cooked and washed up. She washed their clothes in the washing machine.

'Look at us,' she said, 'Mr and Mrs Stereotype. I do the housework. You do the decorating!'

Nathan brought his laptop down from his room and left it on the kitchen table for her to use. He'd set it up so that she could receive and send her own emails.

She rang Jessica every day. She didn't tell her that she'd left the house in Bethnal Green. She let Jessica talk about the things that were going on in St Agnes. Her friend, who had just returned from South America, was staying at the house. She sounded busy. And happy.

Prince and Duke were used to her. They followed her into the living room and fussed around her as she sat on the sofa-bed which had been unfolded for the whole week.

On Thursday night, before they went to sleep Nathan

lay beside her. His pyjamas made him hot so he was on top of the duvet. She was underneath it.

'You know if you did want to talk about it. I'd make a good listener.'

'Talk about it?'

'About what happened here. Ten years ago.'

She didn't answer.

'But you don't have to,' he said.

'I know,' she said.

From beside the bed she could hear one of the dogs turning over, its claws clicking against the wooden floorboards.

She didn't have to get up the next morning. When the dogs started moving round she kept her eyes closed. She felt Nathan getting up. She could hear him padding down the hall and letting them into the back garden. A while later she heard them running back up the hall and into the living room, coming close up to the sofa-bed. She pulled the duvet over her head as Nathan walked towards the windows. He began to unfold the wooden shutters so that the light spilled in. At one point a finger of sunlight seemed to point across the room so that she had to cover her eyes and move to the side.

A funny feeling took hold of her and she must have looked puzzled.

'What's up?' he said.

She noticed he was dressed.

'Nothing,' she said but the shutters had moved

something in her, stirred her thoughts, made her seem distracted.

'There's some juice,' he said, pointing to the floor beside the bed. 'I'm going to take the dogs out.'

'Thanks.'

He leant down to kiss her.

When he went she lay back against the pillows and drank cold orange juice. She stared at the windows. Half of the glass was covered by the wooden shutters. After a while she put her drink down and got out of bed and walked across to them. They were old and splintery. The wood had ridges around the edge and small flower carvings at the corners. It looked bleached. As though the sunlight had penetrated it.

She sat down again, stretching her arms up to the ceiling until she heard her joints crack.

When she lived in the house the shutters had been painted white for a while. She remembered them. Her father had spent many weeks in the living room peeling the paint off. He'd used a kind of torch, she recalled because he'd told her to get away, keep clear, not to touch. *This is hot, Lolly*, he'd said. Sometimes she got closer and watched as the heat made the white paint bubble, like magic. Then he used his scraper to edge it off. It came off in peelings, like slithers of ribbon dropping to the floor. *Don't touch it, Lolly, it's hot.*

But something else was in her mind, something to do with the shutters that was giving her an uncomfortable feeling.

She got up and began to straighten the bedclothes. Now that her Art exam was over she wasn't going to start thinking about stuff again. She picked up her clothes and took them into the cloakroom. She stepped in the shower for a few moments to wake herself up. There was still work to be done. Two separate Drama assignments that needed to be finished by the end of the following week. Then she would go down to Cornwall. As she was drying herself she had an idea. Why not ask Nathan to come down for a couple of weeks? She could show him round, make sure that he was familiar with the area so that when he went to Exeter he would easily be able to find his way over to St Agnes.

She walked back into the living room and picked up her college bag and tipped it up on the bed. She started to sort through her things but every few moments she found herself glancing up at the shutters, looking at them in a questioning way. Inside she felt uneasy and then felt cross. Did she have no control over her own feelings? Was she to be constantly stumbling over past memories?

It was to do with her mother. And the shutters.

She was a little girl watching television and her mother came into the room. It couldn't have been long after the twins' party she thought because she was wearing her sequinned jeans. She was watching some cartoon and had her knees up on the sofa, her fingers running circles around the sparkles that had been stuck onto the denim.

The doorbell rang. Her mum went out and Lauren

expected the front door to open but it didn't. Her mum came back into the room. She was upset. She looked like she was crying. For some reason Lauren didn't remember feeling upset about this. *No, no, no, no*, her mum was saying, walking up and down the room. It was almost as if she was used to seeing her mum upset.

The doorbell rang again. The ring was longer as if someone was holding their finger on the button. Lauren looked at her mother expecting her to go out and see who it was. Instead she just walked up and down and kept saying, *No, no, no*.

Then there was a face at the window. Her mum had her back to the glass and couldn't see it but Lauren knew straight away that it was the clown. His long face and big ears were silhouetted against the glass. Lauren wondered if he had anything interesting in his hands, behind his back. Her mother must have noticed her looking at the window because she turned and saw him. She seemed to freeze and Lauren didn't know what to do but suddenly her mother moved swiftly to the side of the window and began to unfold the shutters, pulling them open, pushing each section of wood firmly over a rectangle of glass, cutting the light off in blocks. She finished one side as the clown knocked gently on the window. Then she pulled the other side shutting out the face that was peering in. *It's all right*, her mum said, *it's no one, it's nothing to worry about.* But it was the middle of the day and the shutters were never normally closed unless it was dark. Then the room was in twilight and the knocking was gone. *It's all right*, her mother said, sitting beside her on the sofa. *Let's watch telly until Daisy wakes up.*

That was the start of her sleeping in her mum's big bed, she on one side, her mum in the middle and Daisy in her cot.

Lauren slumped down on the sofa bed surrounded by the things she'd tipped out of her college bag. The clown again. Why was her mother so upset when he was knocking on the front door? Why was he rising up, thrusting himself into her memory? She hadn't thought about him for ten years. Not until the solicitor mentioned him.

But that wasn't true.

When she'd first looked at the house, all those weeks ago, she had remembered him. Seeing the place had unlocked some door in her head and the clown had come out into her thoughts. Or had it been something else that had nudged her memory of the clown. The assignment that they'd been talking about in Art, *The Child in Play.* Was it talking about childhood and playthings that that had propelled her in the direction of her old house again for the first time in ten years?

Rachel Morris said that a children's entertainer had killed another woman and her child and that her father was using this as a way of getting a new appeal. Did she want to be part of that? How could she be when she still had a clear picture in her head of waking up that day and seeing her father holding the knife that had killed her mum?

Looking down on to the duvet, among her books and pens and text books, she could see the solicitor's card. She picked it up. There was an email address. She could simply send a message saying she did remember a man. She could mention the twins' party. She didn't need to do any more than that. It didn't mean that she believed that her father was innocent. It was just that she needed to tell what she knew. Then the solicitor might leave her alone. Then she could say that she'd done all she could, she could finish her work and pack up and go back to Cornwall.

She could leave Hazelwood Road forever.

And yet being here with Nathan had been such an odd happy time.

The front door opened and she heard the sound of feet running up the hallway. The dogs were back. They came running in, one after the other, their tongues hanging out the sides of their mouths. After circling the sofa-bed a couple of times they headed out towards the kitchen and their food.

'Hi,' Nathan said.

She got up and walked across to him. She put her arms around him and pushed her face into his chest. She put her hands up his T-shirt and onto his bare back.

'Whoa ...' he said, stepping back, smiling, 'just because I haven't got my pyjamas on you shouldn't take advantage of me.'

This was what she liked so much about him. He wasn't all over her. He wasn't *desperate* for things to happen between them.

'What's that?' he said, pointing to the card in her hand.

She looked down at the italicised words *Barrat and Morris Solicitors*. Underneath was the email address.

'Not important. Just someone I've got to contact.'

She went into the kitchen and sat down at the laptop. The email only took moments to write.

*Dear Rachel, I went to a party at the house of a neighbour, Molly Parkes. She had twin daughters and it was their birthday party. There was a children's entertainer there. Molly lives at 53 Hazelwood Road. Lauren Ashe*

She read it over a couple of times.

Then she pressed the *send* button.

# 19

Coming out of college that afternoon she heard a car hooting its horn. A number of people looked round. Lauren was about to look away when a car door opened and Donny got out. He called her name.

'Who's that?' Julie said.

'It's my uncle,' she said, frowning. 'I'll see you later.'

She lowered her head as she crossed the road towards him.

'I've been trying to get in touch for days,' Donny said. 'There's no one at the house!'

She stopped a few metres away from him.

'Where have you been? Where's Jessie?' he said.

'In Cornwall. She's gone home. I'm going back in a couple of weeks.'

'Gone home?'

She nodded.

'What about the house in Bethnal Green? Why aren't you staying there?'

'I'm staying with a friend,' she shrugged.

Lauren moved to let some kids she knew go past. A couple of them said hello and she mumbled replies. Donny was standing behind the driver's door, holding it like a shield. He looked lost for words. She didn't feel like talking to him.

'I have to go,' she said.

'Get in, Lolly,' he said, gesturing towards the car.

She shook her head, 'I've got assignments I have to finish.'

'Please, come and have a coffee somewhere. There's a couple of things I need to talk to you about. Important stuff. Please.'

She sighed.

'There's a café round the corner,' she said.

They sat opposite each other at a large table. Lauren liked the distance between them. She hugged her cup and watched as Donnie drank straight from a bottle of water. On a plate were two cakes, a doughnut and a muffin. Donny knew she liked both sorts. She hadn't touched either of them.

'I've been worried sick about both of you. I went round the house yesterday and there was no sign of anyone. It was like the *Marie Celeste*. Why didn't you tell me you were leaving? Wouldn't that have been fair?'

She stared at him. He was asking for fairness. How many things could she have said in response to that?

'What did you want to talk to me about?' she said, coldly.

'Oh, Lolly, what a mess. We used to be close, you and me.'

He put his hand out, across the table. The end of his finger touched hers. Part of her wanted to move it but all of a sudden she felt weak inside. This was Donny who she had loved. Donny who had taken her surfing and sailing. He had read her stories and played computer games with her. He had bathed her knees when she fell over and slept beside her on her bed when she'd had a nightmare. He played seven card Rummy with her when she'd been broke, letting her win so that she had enough money to go out. A dozen times he'd stayed up late at night foregoing even a can of beer so that he could drive out and pick her up from her friend's house.

And he wasn't even her *dad*.

All of a sudden she thought about her own dad. When she was very young she remembered him sitting on the bed beside her reading a story from a book that she'd chosen. *Not this one again*, he'd say, as if he was peeved. But he wasn't, she knew, because he put on all the voices of the characters. While listening she'd looked at the border round the top of her wallpaper, purple balloons dancing in the air. It made her room seem a joyful place. Her dad sat on the bed beside her reading stories while her eyelids became heavy.

Donny was still talking.

'What happened between me and Jessie, it shouldn't affect you and me,' he said.

She looked up at him. He seemed different. The smooth neat look that he'd had a few weeks back had gone. He had no tie on and his hair had been cut too short. His skin was red as if he had a shaving rash.

'I rang Jessie, but she just won't return my calls.'

Lauren had loved watching him shave when she was younger. It had been like magic. Press the top of a can and white foam appeared. Then it covered his face only to be eaten up by the razor, in broad stripes until there was nothing left, just a few spots like flakes of snow dotted here and there.

'When did she go?' he said.

'What do you want to talk to me about, Donny? I have to go in a minute.'

He looked at her with resignation.

'Two things,' he said. 'A solicitor got in touch with me this morning. She said that you'd contacted her? To help her with your father's appeal?'

Lauren shook her head dismissively.

'She wrote to me. She asked me to go and see her. I only went to tell her to tell my dad . . . My father to back off, to stop sending me letters and stuff. Then she told me about this man who'd been convicted of killing a woman and her children a couple of years later.'

'William Doyle?' Donny said, nodding.

'She asked me if I remembered any children's entertainers.'

'And?'

'I did There was one at a party I went to a couple of houses along. I contacted her to tell her. That was all I did and I told her I didn't want to hear from her any more.'

'So, do you think that this might be important?'

She shook her head, 'How could I have been wrong about what I saw?'

Donny sat back and finished his water.

'This solicitor wants to see me. In case I've remembered anything but I didn't know what to do. Does Jessie know that you went to see her?'

'No. I thought it was better not to say anything. You know what she's like.'

He smiled and for a second it was like old times. Her and Donny agreeing about Jessica.

'Are you going to see the solicitor?' she said, looking away from him.

'I don't know. That's why I came round to see Jessie. Well, that and other reasons.'

'What was the other thing?' she said, brusquely. 'You said you had two things to talk about. What was the other one?'

'Alison had a miscarriage.'

'Oh.'

'It was probably for the best.'

'How do you mean?'

'I'm not sure it was really working out? Alison and me. It was all a bit of a whirlwind. We both got carried along. It takes a while to get to know someone properly.'

Lauren stared at him. Without a tie and with cropped hair he looked rougher. And he had a mildly petulant expression on his face. Like a boy who had lost something. She instantly knew why he'd wanted to speak to her. It was nothing to do with the solicitor. He wanted to know about Jessica. He was gauging whether or not to go back to her. She should have been pleased but it made her feel tired. She pushed her cup away and made as if to leave.

'Don't go,' he said, patting his pockets, making his coins clink. 'I'll get you something else? A sandwich?'

She shook her head and stood up, working her way around the seats and other tables. She left the café. He was only steps behind her.

'Please Lolly, I just need to talk.'

He needed to talk. Why was it always about him? Or Jessica?

'You can drive me to my friend's street. But I don't want to talk about you and Jess.'

He frowned at her.

'I want you to tell me about my mum and dad. Before that day. I need to know more about them. Jess will never say anything about that time.'

'All right,' he said, looking uncomfortable. 'Get in.'

'And I want the truth,' she said, as they drove off, 'I want to know what it was really like.'

They parked a couple of streets from Hazelwood Road. The engine was off and Donny had opened the window on his side to let some air in. Lauren was sitting with her knees tightly together, her hands clasped on her lap. The car felt different, smelled different. Glancing along the dashboard she saw a lighter. Donny was smoking again.

'It was a funny time,' Donny said, 'when Jessie first took me back to Grace's house.'

He was tapping his fingers on the steering wheel. Maybe, at that very moment, he was desperate for a cigarette.

'We'd been together for about six months and she kept saying, *You should come and meet my sister. She's the exact opposite to me.*'

Lauren had a picture of the two women in her head. Her mum seemed tall and Jessica short. But that was because her image of her mum came from when she was a small child always looking up at her. Now she was taller than Jessica by a couple of inches. Would that have been the same for her mum? Would she have been bigger than her own mum, pulling her into her shoulder for a hug? Patting her on the head as she'd done to Jessica many times.

'Grace was ten years older than Jessie but they looked very similar. It was her personality that was so different. She was a very serious woman, didn't smile a lot. She was thinner than Jessie though, actually she was too thin as if she never ate a good meal. Jessie told me that she'd suffered from post-natal depression.'

'I didn't know that,' Lauren said, quickly.

'It was after Daisy was born. She'd had treatment, seemed to be on the mend.'

Lauren knew her mum had been down, she remembered lots of time when her mum was miserable but she'd never thought of it as having a proper name. *post-natal depression* was serious, something to be concerned about. Maybe that's why she was always so *worried* about everything.

'I first met her the Christmas before it happened.'

The Christmas before the summer she and Daisy died.

Her baby sister's first and last Christmas.

'Grace interrogated me. *What's your degree in? Do you think you'll get a 2-1? A first? Where do your parents live? What sort of a job are you intending to get?* It was like she was Jessie's mum and dad rolled into one and she was making sure I was right for her. That was the thing. Since their mum died and their dad moved to Spain, Grace had taken care of Jessie. So she did sort of act like her mother.'

'Daisy was just a small baby?'

'About three months old, I think. Your dad was there then. He didn't say much really, just kept offering me a can of beer. I remember that. Every time there was a gap in the conversation or lunch was over he'd say, *Beer, Don?* He always called me *Don*, not Donny. Maybe he thought Donny was a soppy name.'

Lauren thought about this. Her father had been a builder. His hands had always been rough and calloused, his clothes always dusty and grimy. People called him *Robbie*. Was this more of a man's name than *Donny*?

'Jessie visited your mum a lot but then, roundabout Easter, I think, your dad left again.'

'Again?'

'He'd left your mum before. He liked women. He was in and out of their houses. I think he played around a bit over the years. I got a feeling that the baby was an attempt for them to stay together.'

Lauren felt a sting. She hadn't been enough of a reason for her mum and dad to stay together, they needed a second child.

'Once he left Jessie stayed over there a lot of the time. I was always welcome, Grace said, but I never felt relaxed. There was always some crisis going on. She was depressed. She was on tablets. She couldn't look after the baby. Your dad was coming back. Then he wasn't. Your dad gave her an awful time.'

'Didn't anyone help her? A doctor? A counsellor?'

'Jessie tried to help her. She stayed as much as she could. Actually, it nearly broke us up. Jessie and me, we'd finished our degrees and we'd planned to go to Spain, stay with Jessie's dad, travel round, maybe get some work. Then Jessie changed her mind and said she couldn't leave Grace. I blew my top. I just . . .'

Donny went quiet. He reached across and picked up the lighter. He fiddled with it and looked as though he was on the brink of pulling a packet of cigarettes out of his pocket.

'I often think, if we hadn't gone to Spain, that it wouldn't have happened. We'd have been there and stopped it.'

'How could you?'

'Just by being there. Like as a buffer between Grace and Robbie. Helping Grace get over the fact that Robbie was leaving her for good. If we'd been there maybe we could have stopped the war that was going on between them.'

'I never saw a war going on,' Lauren said.

'No, they would have hidden it. It would have happened when you were in bed or at school or playing with friends. Grace would have made sure that you didn't witness any of the nasty stuff. She adored you and the baby. You were her lifeline. When we went to Spain I remember Jessie saying, *The kids'll get her through this. She loves them more than anything. She'll find the strength to get over that scumbag.*'

'She never got the chance.'

'I remember that we were sitting in a bar on the seafront at Palma and Jessie's dad was running along the promenade towards us. Jessie made a joke about it at first. *What's he doing, silly old buffer*, she said and when he got up to our table I said, *You'll need a beer after that* and he was shaking his head but he couldn't speak because he was out of breath. Then he said, *Something awful's happened.*'

He stopped talking for a few moments. Then he reached across her into the glove compartment and pulled out a packet of cigarettes.

'Needs must,' he said and lit one up, taking a long drag and holding his breath before exhaling out of the window.

*Something awful's happened,* her granddad had said. She hadn't known him very well. She'd met him a few times when he came to England and saw her mum. A tall thin man with white hair cropped short and tanned leathery skin. When she saw him at her mum and Daisy's funeral he'd hugged her so tight she couldn't breathe. A year later he died of a heart attack, Jessica told her. He was lying by his swimming pool and he just died. His wife found him but it was too late for an ambulance. Lauren had felt like she should cry at the time but hadn't managed it.

A ring tone sounded and Donny got his mobile out of his shirt pocket.

'Oh, hi,' he said and holding the mobile away he whispered, 'It's the solicitor.'

He talked for a few moments then cut the call.

'What?' she said.

'The solicitor has been to see one of your old neighbours with photographs of William Doyle. She recognised him. Said it was the same man who did her children's birthday party in May of that year.'

Lauren sat very still.

'This is mad,' Donny said, stubbing out his cigarette on the soul of his shoe and throwing it out of the car window. 'So it was someone else who did it? I don't get it.'

'No, no,' Lauren said, 'I know what I saw.'

She closed her eyes. She tried to remember the scene but it wouldn't come. Instead she tried to picture her father standing with his back to the big double bed looking down at her mum who was slumped up against the wall in a gap between the furniture. It *was* her father because he had half turned and she'd seen his profile and the fact that he was holding a knife. The scene was vague though slipping away from her and then she saw the back of the clown, in his red trousers with the yellow dots and the purple tails of his coat hanging down. Was he there? In the big bedroom?

Could it be, after all this time, that things were not as they had seemed?

'Don't cry, Lolly,' Donny said.

*179*

She looked at him with surprise. She hadn't known she was crying.

# 20

All evening she was anxious. She thought of William Doyle, over and over, the clown who had been at the twins' party. She'd seen him again, afterwards, although she hadn't told this to the solicitor. Once in Woolworth's when she was buying a toy and once he'd come to her door to speak her mum. He'd given her a marble that she'd thought looked like a jewel. Her mum had talked as though she was thinking of having a party. The third time had been different. He'd been ringing her bell and then tapping on the window, his face visible through the glass and it had sent her mum into a panic. She'd closed the living-room shutters blocking him out, blocking the daylight and the world out.

Lauren had never seen him again. Or had she?

She walked up and down in the living room, the dogs following after her. She sat down at the kitchen table tapping her fingers on the surface. She stared out of the window into the garden.

'You all right?' Nathan said.

'Just thinking about my uncle,' she said.

She'd told him about meeting Donny and the miscarriage. She'd kept the rest to herself.

She tried to draw out another memory of William Doyle. She'd gone over it all in her head, hoping that it would trigger something, some other sighting of this man. As if her memory was like a map and going down one road would lead her to other places. Could it be that her mum had gone out with him somewhere, on a kind of date? That she had become involved with him. Could it have happened in June when Donny and Jessie had gone to Spain? Her mum was on her own for three weeks before the murder. A lot could happen in three weeks.

About eight Nathan took hold of her hand and pulled her into the living room and sat her on the bed.

'What's up?' he said, biting his lip.

'Just stuff,' she said.

'The house?' he said. 'Being here?'

'Partly. But not really. I can't explain. It's complicated.'

'Is it me? Are you fed up with me?' he said.

'No, it's not you.'

'If you want to finish it . . .'

'I don't want to finish it,' she said, a squeak of exasperation in her voice. 'I've told you it's personal. It's about my family.'

'I can't help if you don't tell me about it.'

She shook her head. She simply couldn't lay it all out in front of him. Or anyone.

'Maybe it would help. If you told me about it. Confided in me.'

She was instantly annoyed. Did he want the *details*? Was that it?

'I don't *want* to talk about it,' she said, sharply, 'I've told you before, I don't *talk* about it. If that's the only reason you asked me to stay then I might as well go. If you want to find out what happened to my family you'll have to do it on the internet! You won't find out from me!'

'Whoa!' he said, putting his hands up as if in surrender. 'Is that what you think? That I asked you to stay to find out about your past?'

'You did say you were researching the house. As I remember, you said, *I need to know everything that happened in this house.* Is that why I'm staying here? So that you can know everything?'

'I can't believe you said that.'

He said the words dully. He stood up. The dogs sat up and looked expectantly at him.

'I'm taking the dogs out,' he said.

She couldn't answer him. She listened to the front door shutting and felt her shoulder blades stiffen with frustration. Why was this happening to her? Why couldn't things be simple? Hadn't she had enough drama in her life?

And then there was Donny. He wasn't having a baby any more. In fact it sounded as though Donny and his new woman were finished. Jessica should know about it. Lauren should email her or ring her. But if she did Jessica would jump on the next train and come back to London and she didn't want that. Not while all this other stuff was going on with the solicitor.

She didn't know what to do.

After a while she went into the kitchen and sat at the laptop. She looked through Nathan's files wondering if he had kept the stuff she'd seen weeks before on the first day that she came into his house. As her eye scrolled down she noticed a file marked *House History*. She pressed the *open* icon.

There was the newspaper report from ten years before that she had seen.

Friday 23rd June. **House of Death** Mother and child murdered in Hazelwood Road. Seven-year-old survives carnage. The police are urgently seeking Robert Slater, husband and father.

She read over the article, slowly this time, taking it all in.

Police officers were shocked by the grisly scene they witnessed in a house on Hazelwood Road in East London. Mother of two, Grace Slater, and her nine-month-old baby were found dead at just after seven am on Monday morning. Police officers found the family in a first floor bedroom.

Sources say that the alarm was raised by Ms Slater's seven-year-old daughter, who survived. It is thought that someone tried to kill both children and was interrupted by the children's mother, who later died of a single stab wound. A police statement will be issued today.

She scanned down and read a couple of other reports which said the same things in different ways. Then she saw a different kind of report. Not from a newspaper but possibly a magazine or a Sunday supplement. She looked at the date. It had been written nine months later, after the trial of her father. It was headed **Why Do Men Kill Their Families?**

It was long, too long to read it all. She skimmed over the first few paragraphs until she found her father's name.

The case of Robert Slater is, some would argue, a textbook example of why some men are *driven* to kill their families. The prosecution suggested that Grace Slater had goaded Robert Slater into his actions telling him that she would take the children away to live in Spain with her family and that he would never see them again. In his despair and rage Robert Slater turned up at his family's home in the middle of the night and argued with his wife. This led to him smothering one of his children and attempting to do the same with the other. During this sequence of events he also killed his wife with a single stab wound. It's yet another classic case of familicide.

The way in which the crime is carried out is indicative of the relationships involved. In some cases, when fathers kill their families, the act itself is brutal and thorough suggesting that the father is in a blind rage and cannot stop once he has started. This often ends in the suicide of the father. Other cases though show an almost uncertain, faltering approach to the crime itself as if the victim is half-hearted about what he is doing. Part of him wants to kill but another part of him is completely aware that he is killing those who he loves.

The case of Robert Slater is an example of this *tentative* approach to murder. He smothered his baby daughter but did not manage to kill his seven-year-old. He stabbed his wife only once and pathologists argued that this wound was not deep and did not bring about sudden death. Grace Slater died from her injuries rather than the violence of the stab wound. Robert Slater then ran from the scene, evading police capture for four days until he eventually gave himself up.

Robert Slater is still in denial. He claims that he found the bodies and attempted to come to the aid of his dying wife. He says he removed the knife from her chest and tried to stem the bleeding but it was too late. Robert Slater testified that he had no idea that his eldest daughter was alive.

Robert Slater has started a life sentence and must come to terms with what he has done.

The article continued discussing other cases. Lauren's eye went back to the top and read it over again. Jessica had told her many years before that her father said that he was trying to help her mother, not kill her.

Was there a faint possibility that he was telling the truth?

She accessed Google and put the words *William Doyle* and *Murder* into the search engine. Within seconds she was faced with line after line of matches. She didn't open any of them. She just let her eyes sweep down the page.

**William Doyle Convicted of Murdering Rochester Family**

**William Doyle Gets Life for Rochester Slayings**

**Life Means Life for William Doyle.** *Mother and Child killed in own home.*

Most of them were from four years before but there was a newer one halfway down.

**DNA links William Doyle, Convicted Murderer, with second Killing.** *Mother and Baby found dead in bedroom in Bournemouth.*

She was still reading when she heard the front door and the patter of feet on the floorboards. The dogs came running in, their tails wagging, their fur wet from swimming in the lake. Nathan was behind them. He avoided looking at her.

'I'm sorry,' she said. 'I want you to look at this. Then you'll know why I'm in a state.'

'No, it's all right. You've got your right to privacy. I understand that.'

'Please. I know you're annoyed at me but if you look at this you might understand.'

He wavered. Then he came across and pulled another kitchen chair out and sat down beside her. For a long time he was quiet, reading the headings on the page. When she told him who William Doyle was and how he was connected to her family he started to open the documents.

Later he clicked off the laptop and stood up.

'Come on, let's go out and get some food.'

But she was crying again. The second time in hours. The tears blinked out easily and she wiped them away with the edge of her hand. He pulled her up by her elbow.

'Some Chinese I think and a few drinks. You need to get away from all this stuff for a few hours.'

She nodded.

She went with him. She put her hand in his and they walked out of the house towards the car.

# 21

It was past midnight before they went to bed. On the floor were several spent cans of beer and an empty bottle of sparkling wine. Lauren had drunk a lot. The wine, sweet and fizzy, had gone down like lemonade. It had made her feel light and breezy, trouble free. They'd talked about her family for a long time. Then he'd asked her about her life in Cornwall and about her plans.

Now they lay facing each other in bed. Nathan kissed her a few times and she hugged him tightly. He was wearing another pair of his dad's pyjamas. These had longer legs which he'd had to roll up. She could feel the fabric unrolling with her feet. She began to giggle.

He kissed her again for a long time. She felt her skin softening, her chest rising and falling, her hair falling across her face.

'I wonder what my friends would say if they knew that I was in bed with a mermaid,' he said, weaving his fingers through her hair.

She spluttered out a laugh.

'I make you laugh. That's one good thing.'

'There are lots of good things,' she said, immediately

serious, her arm slipping round him pulling him towards her.

He kissed her again, his hands running up and down her back. He put his mouth to her ear and she could hear him breathing.

'I've got condoms,' he whispered.

'Not here,' she said. 'Not in this house.'

It sounded like *thish house* and she found herself giggling at her words even though she'd meant them seriously.

'I'm sorry, I know it's not funny,' she said.

Nathan went to say something and then stopped. It was quiet for a moment, so quiet that she could almost hear him thinking.

'It's definitely not meant to be *funny*,' he said. 'Maybe when I come to Cornwall? . . .'

'You can bring your condoms,' she said, spluttering a laugh.

'Maybe you'll manage to stop laughing by then.'

'Sorry!'

It sounded like *shorry* and she clamped her hand over her mouth afraid that she would start again.

He turned round and she put her arm around his chest. The night had seemed like it was ruined but he had made it better, cheered her up. None of it was her fault, he'd said. She just had to try and remember things in her own time and contact the solicitor if she wanted to. Whatever happened she had to remember that she had only been seven years old. She had been a victim. It was up to her father to prove his own innocence.

Nathan had also agreed to come to St Agnes for a couple of weeks in the summer. It gave her a good feeling and she lay for a while, her arm around him, thinking about the places she would take him to visit. Her eyelids were heavy and she was feeling sleepy from the alcohol. She heard Nathan's breathing becoming regular. After a few moments she knew he was asleep.

She lay there for a while staring into the darkness. She felt woozy, sure that at any moment she would go to sleep. Her mouth was dry though and there was something restless inside her. She turned away from Nathan and stared at the dogs who were lying close together. She closed her eyes and tried to blank her thoughts out so that she could slip into sleep but the effort of trying was keeping her awake. She felt like she wanted to laugh but didn't. She had definitely had too much to drink. Not as bad as the night that Julie and Ryan came round. Still, though, her mouth was dry. She looked round and saw that Nathan had thrown the sheet off and was lying on his back. He was completely still. She put her hand out and let it rest briefly on his rib cage. She felt it rise and fall. She lay back. It was pitch dark and there were no sounds from outside in the street.

She picked her mobile off the floor and saw that it was 1:07am.

She was thirsty.

She got up out of the bed carefully, trying not to disturb Nathan. As she moved she heard the thump, thump, thump of one of the dog's tails on the floor. The other one was fast asleep and she stepped across him, pulled her jeans on under her nightie and went out to the kitchen. Without turning the light on she got a glass of water. She had a few mouthfuls of it and put it down. After a few moments Prince joined her and she patted his head, her feet feeling the cool of the terracotta tiles.

William Doyle came back into her thoughts. It made her mood dip.

Why had her mum pulled the shutters over when he was outside? Had she been afraid of him? Was that why she took Lauren to sleep in the big bed. Because she'd wanted them all together, safety in numbers?

She took another sip of the cold water.

Something was forming in her head. It was an uncomfortable idea but she didn't seem to be able to dismiss it. She should go up to her mum and dad's bedroom. To look at it. To see if *being* there might remind her of things that had become hazy and vague in her mind. All the things she'd been thinking about had happened in that room. Could she actually go up *there*? Surely it was unthinkable.

She turned to the window and looked out into the garden. The sky was lighter in colour than the trees and bushes. It looked cloudy but she could see a brighter spot. It was probably a full moon sending silver beams through the clouds. She heard the sound of feet and looked around. Duke had come out and Prince was sniffing at him, his tail wagging. They both stood at the back door. She put her glass down and opened it. The dogs dashed out and disappeared in and out of bushes, their honey-coloured coats standing out among the shadows on the night.

It was warm. She stretched her arms up to the sky and walked out onto the patio. Turning back she looked at the house. The back of it had changed. She only remembered one door opening from the kitchen into the garden but now there was a long sleek window and two French doors.

Then the dogs were fussing around her legs and she went back inside and closed the door as quietly as she could. She stood very still in the kitchen as a strange reckless feeling took hold of her. It propelled her out into the hallway, her bare feet hardly touching the floorboards. She paused for a second to hear if there were any signs that Nathan was awake. There were none. She came to the foot of the stairs. She clicked the light on and looked up towards the first floor landing.

It was only a room.

In ten years other people had lived there. They had slept, eaten, watched TV; they had laughed, cried, rowed, made up; they had filled it with noise and been at ease with its silence.

It was not a place to fear. It was a place for her to reclaim.

Her mouth was dry as dust as she took a deep breath and put her foot on the stairs.

# 22

She stood at the door nervously. She considered turning the light on but there was no need. There was a streetlamp outside and it shone in through the net curtains throwing a watery glow across the room. When she had lived there long maroon velvet curtains had hung down each side of the windows. In the bay there had been an old fashioned wooden chest on which sat her mother's doll's house. The curtains could only be partially drawn because the doll's house was in the way. It meant that at night the streetlight shone in and in the early mornings natural light seeped into the room.

Unlike the rest of the house it hadn't changed. The bed was opposite the bay window, its headboard against a flat wall. On one side of it was the old fireplace. That was the side where Daisy's cot used to be. On the other side had been a huge old fashioned wardrobe and chest of drawers which took up most of the wall.

Now the bay was empty. There was a wardrobe on the side wall but it was small and modern and by it were a number of white plastic see-through boxes stacked on top of each other. All were full up with clothes or books or picture frames.

She walked across and looked out of the window. The street was completely empty. Moving her head at an angle she could see down into the front garden where there was a cat sitting on top of the wheelie bin. Was it the same one that she had seen when she came before? The ginger cat? She thought then of Cleopatra and her kittens. It gave her an ache, a longing to be down in Cornwall with Jessica. For a second she felt tearful and lonely. What was she doing in this house?

In the distance she could hear the faint sound of traffic. In London it was always there, sometimes nearby, sometimes far away. It St Agnes it was the sea she could always hear. Some times the waves were close and loud, crashing against the sea wall. At other times, when the tide was out, the sound was distant and soft.

Turning back she looked at the bed. There were no sheets on it, just the duvet folded back and some pillows without pillowcases. When she'd lived in the house her mother's bed had always been neatly made up. Her quilt had been silky and there had been small fancy cushions that had to be taken off the bed before they went to sleep. *They're just for show*, her mum had said.

She straightened the quilt, smoothing the corners. She plumped up the pillows. Then she sat down. She only paused for a moment before she let herself lay back, her head on the pillow looking up at the ceiling, in the place where she had lain ten years before.

She closed her eyes. She felt light-headed from the drink.

It had always been a treat to sleep in her mum's bed. When she was ill or needed cheering up the big bed was a refuge. Waking up in the middle of the night with a hot sore throat or tummy ache she would call out for her mum or dad and one of them would come padding along the hallway and scoop her up and take her into the bed between them. When Daisy came it had stopped. If she was unwell or if she woke up after a bad dream her dad would come down to her room and lay on her bed until she dozed off to sleep. Daisy had priority in the big bedroom. When her dad left home she sometimes slept in her mum's room but it wasn't as nice. Her mum kept telling her to shush in case she woke Daisy. *Don't sniff. Stop wriggling.* Mostly she stayed in her own bed. Sometimes Jessica came down the stairs from the attic and sat by her, reassuring her or telling her stories.

Yet on one day that summer (she thought it was the day of the shutters) she began to sleep in her mum's bed every night. *Just the three of us. It will be cosy*, her mum had said.

How long had that gone on for? A week? Two weeks?

She turned on her side pulling the pillow into her neck and thought about those days.

She always woke early. The daylight edged into her mum's room and usually unsettled her. She tried to lay still but often just got out of the bed and went across to the doll's house and played silently. She looked through the tiny windows at the household inside. It wasn't possible to move anything so she had to use her imagination. There were two figures at the dining-room table. The woman was wearing a long dress and had her hair up at the back in a bun. The man had a black suit on. They were sitting across from each other and she imagined them having conversations about the children, who, she saw, flicking her eye up to the upstairs of the house, were tucked into bed. After a while she pictured the woman's hand moving across the table towards the man and the man grasping it and smiling. Sometimes she focused on the kitchen where a maid was standing by a stove. The maid was all in black with a frilly white cap. On the kitchen table were pots and pans. The maid would move soon, she thought and pick up one of the pots to use on the stove. She looked and looked. There never was any movement but in her mind the maid did seem to turn and reach out to pick up one of the pots.

These stories never got very far. From behind Lauren heard the snuffles of Daisy as she began to wake and the build up of a cry that would alert her mum and start the day. *You're not at the doll's house again, Lauren? Careful with it,* her mum would say, *it's not a toy it's an antique. It's not really for playing with.*

And yet hadn't she seen her mum playing with it herself?

Lauren opened her yes. Then she sat up on Nathan's parents' bed. It was an effort but she moved the pillows so that they made a backrest and she sat staring into the empty bay window. Something was making her feel excited and uncomfortable at the same time. She *had* seen her mum play with the doll's house.

It was late at night she remembered. The room was dark and the only light was coming from outside in the street. She had seen her mum in the bay window sitting cross-legged by the doll's house. It was opened and she seemed to be playing with the figures and furniture. Daisy was still in her cot and the space beside her had been empty. The duvet was ruffled as if her mum had been sleeping there but now she was up, sitting at the old chest playing with the doll's house.

It had been the *middle* of the night. She'd known because of the silence in the street and the absolute stillness of the house. Her mum was in her white nightdress sitting down by the doll's house and moving things around. There'd been a low whisper as though her mum was talking to herself. Maybe she was making up stories about the people in the house just the way Lauren did.

Lauren remembered it as if it was yesterday. She let the image play over in her head as her eyelids drooped. Her head was heavy with alcohol, her mouth paper dry. She felt herself slipping down the pillows. She had drunk too much and would probably have a headache in the morning. She closed her eyes and her thoughts fragmented and her mind relaxed and she sunk into sleep.

It was only a dream. The room was only just light. Lauren was a little girl of seven lying listening to morning sounds, the birds and the distant cars and a door shutting a few houses up. It was only a dream though, she knew it as she was lying there. She was in her mum's bed, and the strange thing was that Cleopatra was there curled up beside her. There were no kittens, but Jessica was sitting on the end of the bed cuddling Daisy. From downstairs she could hear someone moving about, a man. The footsteps were heavy as though he was stamping his feet. Doors opened and closed. Jessica must have seen the worry on her face because she said, *It's only Slater*. Lauren frowned. She didn't like when Jessica called her dad *Slater*. She couldn't see her mum and Daisy was beginning to make a moaning noise. She lifted herself up to look but had to nudge off a pillow that was half over her head. The space beside her was empty so her mum had already got up out of bed. The footsteps were continuing downstairs. The man was walking up and down, up and down. It was making her feel uneasy as though he was annoyed at her and it would only be a matter of time before he came upstairs his footsteps getting louder on each step.

But wait, in the dream, her mum *was* in the room. She was at the doll's house playing with the furniture and the figures. The front of the doll's house was open and her mum was kneeling down at it. She was taking things out, laying them on the floor, fiddling about, putting things back, tiny chairs and tables and a maid all in black with a white frilly cap.

Cleopatra had stood up and was looking straight at her. The cat's eyes were getting closer and closer and it made Lauren want to move back out of the way, only the bed head was behind her, hard and solid so she had to stay where she was. Cleopatra's eyes were huge, as big as a person's. She looked closely at Lauren then moved up and circled until she was sitting by her face. Lauren could feel the heat of her and wished she would go away. She could still hear the sound of the man walking about downstairs. She was sure he was directly underneath her, putting one foot after another onto the wooden floors, walking this way and that, opening the living-room door and slamming it closed, coming to the bottom of the stairs and turning away back down to the kitchen. Stamp, stamp stamp. Lauren turned to the side, her face was pushing into the cat's fur. She heard it purring, a low insistent sound. Or maybe it was the other way round. The cat was edging itself closer to her, its body uncurling across her face and neck, cutting out the light. Get away from me, she wanted to say but the cat's head turned suddenly and the green eyes stared at her pinning her to the pillow. She had to close her mouth and hold her breath because the cat was bearing down on her and she didn't like the feel of it near her mouth.

In the dream the footsteps had stopped for a moment but all of a sudden they began again. They were coming up the stairs rapidly, speeding up. Lauren could feel the vibrations on each stair and in her head the noise was getting louder and louder and she needed to breathe but she couldn't. She brought her hands up to her face to push the cat away, to get it off her mouth so that she could get some air but the steps were outside the room on the landing, heavy boots marching towards her.

The door opened as she pushed the cat off and she turned to look.

A clown was standing there.

A white face with red nose and red lips. She didn't speak. She looked around wildly but Jessica was gone. It was just her mum kneeling at the doll's house. It looked as though she had a piece of paper in her hand. *Go to sleep now, Lauren*, she said. And when she looked back to the door the clown was gone and it was her dad. *What do you want, Robbie?* her mum said. But Lauren knew that the clown was coming back, she could sense the footsteps as they moved through the house, padding along the landing, shoving the door open.

She struggled to sit up. She had to sit up. The clown was coming back into the room. She had to get up, to call to her mum, to shout out but somehow she just lay there, the cat pining her down. She was powerless. She knew the door was opening and saw, out the corner of her eye, a hand emerging holding something.

Scarves, all different colours, spilling from the clown's hands.

She'd thought it would be a knife. She closed her eyes and began to cry. She opened her mouth to scream out but nothing came.

'Lauren, Lauren, wake up. What are you doing up here?'

A hand was shoving at her shoulder.

She woke up, her head twisting from side to side.

The darkness of the bedroom was cool and calm. She

looked around. She was alone on the bed. Nathan was sitting beside her. She turned to the door. No clown. No cat. No one. Just her dreams. Just a stupid dream.

She let out a gasping sob. She pulled herself up to a sitting position, her heart pounding.

'What's wrong? Why did you come up here? I thought you didn't want to come up here.'

Nathan looked bewildered.

'I had to,' she said, her eyes brimming with water, her nose running.

'I don't get it.'

'I had to see if I remembered anything new. I must have fallen asleep. I had a bad dream. It's probably the drink. I don't know.'

'Come on, come downstairs. I never meant for you to come up here.'

He led her out of the room. She let him take her hand as if she was small child. As the door closed behind her she remembered her mother sitting at the doll's house playing with the figures. That had been real. Not part of the dream. Her mother had sat down at the doll's house and played with it. She was sure.

# 23

She woke up on the sofa-bed. Her head was heavy and she raised herself onto her elbow looking for her mobile. It was on the floor. She picked it up. It was ten past eleven. She sat up quickly. For a second she'd thought it was a college day but it was Saturday. She pulled her hair back into a tie, tucking stray strands behind her ears. There was a patter of feet as the dogs came in, their tails wagging feverishly, as if they hadn't seen her for weeks. She patted each of them in turn, managing a half-smile.

Nathan followed them into the room.

'Hi,' she said.

'How are you feeling?' he sat down on the bed beside her.

'A bit rough,' she said, her hand on her forehead, 'Thanks for looking after me. I don't usually get into such a state. It was being up there in that room.'

He nodded. He was biting his lip and looked worried.

'It's my fault. Maybe you shouldn't have stayed here.'

'No, it's been good – me being here. I've remembered such a lot. It will upset me. It's bound to. But it's better to know, isn't it?'

'I suppose so.'

'I'll tell you what though, I do hold you to blame for one thing.'

'What?'

'My headache. All that alcohol. That's your fault.'

'I'll sort out the aspirin.'

In the shower she stood for a while letting the hot water soak over her. It had been a bad night and yet inside she felt as though she'd taken a giant step forward. She'd gone into her parents' room. She'd even slept there for a while. Too much drink had given her a feeling of bravado and she'd used it to step into the past.

She'd had a bad dream. It had shaken her and confused her. It had been a kind of pick and mix of all the things that had been occupying her mind in the last weeks. Somewhere in the heart of it had been a sort of truth though. She *had* heard the footsteps coming up to the bedroom. Had she felt afraid when she was seven years old? She had felt unsettled and apprehensive but how could she have known what was to come? The fear in her dream was there because now, ten years later, she knew what the footsteps meant, what had happened when that door opened. Her knowledge of William Doyle had rewritten her memories.

A clown with red lips and ears that stuck out. She'd known nothing of this at the time. She'd seen him in Woolworth's, at her front door, at her window but she hadn't *understood* anything. She was a child. She'd only seen a tiny bit of a much bigger picture. It was as if she was looking through the keyhole of a room and just seeing a fraction of what was happening in there.

Now she thought she understood. Her mum had started a relationship with this man, William Doyle, and become terribly afraid of him.

Underneath all these thoughts there was a feeling of hope that she hardly dared to acknowledge. Like a thin candle in a dark room, a feathery flame that barely gave out any light. There was a chance that her dad, Robert Slater, could be innocent. It was something she'd fought against for ten years. That tiny possibility that she might have been wrong. That what she saw was in fact her dad *discovering* his murdered family.

Nathan had been there for her. He had popped into her life suddenly and surprisingly. She'd only met him because of her interest in the house, because of what had happened to her. Something good had come out of Hazelwood Road.

She washed and rinsed herself. When she turned the shower off she felt suddenly cold, her skin rising in goose pimples. She dried herself and got dressed quickly. In the kitchen Nathan had laid some stuff on the table; butter, jam and honey. There was a smell of toast in the air and in spite of her head throbbing she felt hungry.

'Here's the aspirin,' he said, handing her the packet and putting a rack of toast on the table.

She took two and a drink of juice.

'Are you going to talk to your aunt about it?'

She sat down at the table and frowned. She took a piece of toast and buttered it. Underneath her feeling of relief was a dark ripple, an undercurrent of worry. How would Jessica react to the fact that she was going to go to her dad's solicitor's to tell them things that would help him in his appeal. *As far as I'm concerned he's dead and buried*, Jessica had said, only weeks before.

'I don't know,' she said, taking a bite of the toast.

'She has to know. And what about your uncle? I know he doesn't live with you any more but didn't you say he was like a dad?'

She nodded, 'I don't mind telling Donny. He's always been easier to talk to than Jess.'

'But you will have to tell her at some point.'

'I'll be back in Cornwall next week. Nothing will happen before then. It'll be better if I tell her face to face. In any case it may all come to nothing. This William Doyle may not be involved at all. These things I've remembered, they might not change anything. I'll wait until I hear something from the solicitor's. There's no point in upsetting Jessica if it all is going to come to nothing.'

They were quiet for a moment. She ate her toast hungrily.

'I've got to go into work today. Do you want to come and meet me? At about six? We could go out somewhere?' Nathan said.

'That sounds good. This afternoon I'll go back home and start to pack up some of my stuff for Cornwall? That way I won't have so much to do next week.'

'So I'll see you at the museum? At six?'

She nodded, her mouth too full to speak.

After he went she tidied up the breakfast things. Then she packed some of her stuff in a bag.

Before leaving she went upstairs and opened the door to her parents' old bedroom. The sun was shinning in through the net curtains and the room was light and warm. The bed was rumpled from where she'd been in it. The walls were painted a beige colour and the frames of the windows had been sanded. The floorboards were bare although they hadn't been sanded or polished.

She walked in.

It was just a room. Just four walls with furniture. It had no memory of the past no sense of what had happened here. She straightened the bed, pulling back the duvet so that the mattress aired. Then she puffed up the pillows.

Downstairs she got her bag and left.

# 24

The house in Bethnal Green smelled stale. She walked round opening the windows. Then she went up to her room and turned her computer on. She wrote an email to Rachel Morris listing the things that she had remembered about the clown. She tried to be as full in her descriptions as she could. She said nothing about her dad. Any hint that she was changing her story or reinterpreting what she saw would give too much hope. If her dad was going to prove his innocence it had to be without her help. She saw what she saw.

Also she kept thinking about Jessica.

Jessica's hatred for Lauren's dad had never abated, in fact it had probably strengthened as time passed. When Donny left it tipped Jessica upside down. If it turned out that her sister's husband was innocent then it would be another emotional upheaval for her and she would go into freefall. She would have ten years of ingrained loathing to deal with. Lauren dreaded it. She would tell Jessica about it, but not until she was absolutely certain that there was real evidence against William Doyle.

A noise from downstairs made her look round. The front door was opening. She stood up and went out onto the landing. It was Donny standing sheepishly in the hallway. On the floor, by his feet were some bags.

'Hi, Lolly,' he said with an embarrassed shrug.

She frowned and then in an instant she knew why he was there. She'd been right all those weeks ago when she told Jessica to give him time. She went down the stairs quickly and walked up to him. Without a word she put her arms around his chest and hugged him.

Donny had come home.

'I didn't think you'd be here,' he said, sitting across the kitchen table.

They were both drinking black tea. There was no milk. There was nothing much in the fridge at all. Donny had put his bags in his room but he hadn't unpacked. His car keys were sitting on the table beside him as though he wasn't quite sure if he was staying.

'I'm going down to St Agnes,' he said.

She frowned.

'I want to see Jessie. I want to sort it all out. I don't know if I've left it too late.'

'Does she know you're coming?'

He shook his head.

'Why don't you come with me?' he said after a moment

'I don't want to be in the middle of another emotional thing with you and Jess. It's better if you sort it out yourselves.'

'I'll be honest. I'm frightened she might shut the door in my face. If you come with me she won't.'

He was looking at her in a pleading way.

'I don't know,' she said.

'Think about it. I'm going to have a shower and go in about an hour. We could be down in St Agnes by about seven?'

She left him in the kitchen. Now she was torn. He was back and she was glad of it but she had all this other stuff going on. The solicitor and her email. Nathan who was expecting to meet her at the museum. Her final assignments which had to be in college by next week. Then she had to pack everything up and go back to St Agnes for good. It wasn't a good time to dash off for a weekend, even to help Donny out.

She went to her computer and saw that she had a new message.

*Dear Ms Ashe, Thank you so much for this information. It gives us a much clearer picture of what might have happened. You've been very detailed but I wonder, could we possibly meet up? I'm very busy over the next couple of weeks with other cases but, would it be too much trouble, if I were to come and see you at your home? Tomorrow maybe? Just to clarify a few things?*

*Rachel Morris*

*P.S. Is there any message that you'd like to send to Robert Slater?*

She deleted it immediately. She stiffened her back and looked crossly at the computer screen. No she didn't want to see Rachel Morris and she had no message to send. She just wanted to be left alone. She'd done as much as she could do. She'd teased these memories out, going over and over them so that they built into a kind of picture.

That was all. She wanted nothing more to do with it. Why couldn't they understand that?

She heard Donny along the landing in the shower. He'd put the radio on and changed the channel to a sports programme. A male voice was commentating on a football match. His words were clipped and fast and full of emotion and in the background she could hear the cheer of the crowd.

She sat on her bed and looked around the room. It was tiny in comparison to the rooms in Hazelwood Road. In just six days she'd got used the high ceilings and the space. She'd also got used the patter of the dogs' feet on the wooden floors as they followed her or Nathan around. She'd become comfortable being around Nathan, hearing his jokes, watching him work on the house, feeling at ease with him physically; hugging him, touching him whenever he was near. She wanted to go back and be with him, not be stuck in the middle of Donny and Jessica again.

The bathroom door had opened. She knew this because the football commentary had got louder. And there was the faint aroma of deodorant or after shave. She liked it. It reminded her of times in Cornwall. The pattern of their lives had been the same every morning. Jessica got up first and went downstairs for a large, strong cup of tea. Donny used the bathroom, his radio echoing on the tiled walls. It always woke her up but she never minded. Donny would shave and shower. Sometimes he would argue with the radio as she lay in bed and listened.

Then, when he'd finished she would go into the bathroom next and find it steamy and full of scents. At some point Jessica would call up to Lauren telling her the time. As Lauren came out of the bathroom Donny might emerge from his bedroom, dressed in his work clothes. *Am I good looking or what?* he'd sometimes say and she'd say, *Or what.*

Why had that changed?

She found herself swallowing back, but there was a lump in her throat that she couldn't move. If they had stayed in Cornwall none of this bad stuff would have happened. But then her memories of Hazelwood Road would have stayed the same. And she would never have met Nathan.

Donny was on the landing. She could hear his keys clinking. She made a decision.

'Wait,' she said, picking up a bag and shoving some things into it, 'I'm coming with you.'

'Great,' Donny said, 'you and me, we'll sort this thing out. Maybe we'll bring Jessica back with us.'

Lauren didn't answer. She remembered Jessica's happy emails from St Agnes. She had a new job and an old friend had turned up. Donny didn't know these things. She decided not to tell him. He would find out soon enough.

# Part Four

# House of Secrets

# 25

St Agnes had a festival feel. The streets had bunting flapping from side to side and the flower baskets that hung from shops were overflowing with colours. Balloons hung in twos and threes from lampposts and were blown about by a light breeze. The sun was low and people looked hot and contented. Families were strolling along carrying coolboxes and hanging on to pushchairs laden with beach mats and lilos. Small children were walking alongside rubbing their eyes with the backs of their hands looking dazed. There were bare chests and legs and lots of pink shoulders. Groups of teens languidly moved along, taking great swathes of the pavement up. Lauren looked keenly at them to see if there was anyone she knew.

'Traffic's not too bad,' Donny said.

She nodded. They'd not spoken much on the journey. Donny's face had been concentrated on the road, his hands clamped to the wheel, music radio filling the quiet. Early on in the journey she'd sent a long text to Nathan explaining the situation. She told him she'd be back the next day. After a while he answered *See you tomorrow*. It was brief and a bit curt. She thought he was probably upset by the sudden way in which she had gone. A while later she sent a text saying *Miss you already*. He replied saying *Looking forward to tomorrow*. She felt better.

They only made one stop at a garage where they'd used the toilet and bought sandwiches and soft drinks and sat eating them as the motorway traffic shot past, most of it a blur. Then they'd got back in the car and Donny put his foot down and they seemed to sweep through Somerset and Devon towards Cornwall.

The air conditioning had been on the whole journey but now Lauren pressed a button and the passenger window slid down. Immediately she could smell chips and candyfloss and in amongst it all the briny smells of the sea. There was noise too; chatter and laughter and music that spilled out of a shop. A baby was crying from a stationary pushchair. It was a loud wail that was ignored by its mother who was holding a cigarette between two fingers and inhaling deeply, a look of absolute calm on her face.

They turned off the high street towards the edge of the town. Just another couple of hundred metres and they would turn into Lighthouse Hill and pull up outside their house. Lauren turned her head as a couple of kids she knew walked by on the other side of the street. She felt a pang of recognition, a sense of coming home. It was a surprise. She hadn't expected to feel like this.

The car pulled in suddenly before they got to the turning. It stopped completely and Donny sat for a moment.

'What's wrong?' Lauren said.

'Nerves,' Donny said.

'You've come all this way.'

'I don't know how she'll be. Whether she'll forgive me. Whether she'll have me back. After everything . . .'

Lauren thought of the night when she'd followed Jessica to Donny's flat. Jessica was striding ahead in her petrol-blue dress, her high heels making her taller and more fragile than she had been before. All that passion had driven her forward and she had crashed head on into Donny's new life, his trendy apartment and his new baby. Jessica had walked out of there bruised and broken, the dress wilting against her thin body.

'What do you think?' Donny said, looking at her.

He wanted her to reassure him, to give him confidence.

'I just don't know,' she said, shrugging her shoulders.

A few moments later they pulled up outside the house. A couple of the upstairs windows were open and the net curtains were billowing in and out. Lauren guessed that the windows at the back of the house were open as well. Jessica was always doing that on hot days and it meant that the room doors were forever slamming, making them all jump out of their skins.

'You go ahead,' Donny said, locking the car, looking up at the house with gritted teeth.

Lauren would usually have opened the door with her key but that was back in her bedroom in Bethnal Green. It hadn't occurred to her to bring it. Donny made no attempt to get his key out. She rang the bell. Footsteps came along the hallway and she braced herself for

Jessica's surprised look when she saw them both there.

The door opened. It was a tall man with long yellow hair, some of it in thin plaits.

'Who are you?' Donny said, abruptly, rudely.

Jessica came up behind him. She looked at them both and her eyes narrowed.

'It's all right Zak. This is Donny and Lauren,' she said, addressing her comments to the man.

'Who is *he*?' Donny said, his voice an octave higher.

'Sorry, I haven't introduced you. This is Zak, an old mate from my uni days. He's travelling through so I said he could stay for a while.'

'He's staying?' Donny said, his voice squeaking.

'Can we come in?' Lauren said, feeling a little exposed on the doorstep.

'Course!'

'I'll see you later,' Zak said. 'Good to meet you guys,' he added with a gracious wave of his hand.

'Have a good evening,' Jessica called, as Zak sidestepped them all and went down the path. Lauren noticed that he had wooden clogs on. They made a clip clop sound on the paving stones.

As they went into the house Donny was mumbling about the journey and Jessica mouthed a silent question at Lauren. *What's happening?* Lauren shook her head. It wasn't up to her to say anything.

Lauren left the two of them in the living room and went upstairs. On the landing there were plastic boxes that were full of magazines and the ladder from the loft was down. She moved round it and went along to Jessica and Donny's room. Glancing in she saw three brown cardboard boxes stacked up in the corner. She stepped inside as Cleopatra leapt off the bed and came to her feet. Lauren bent down to stroke the cat. She wondered where the kittens were.

It had been five months since she'd been in this house. It looked different. It *was* different. Jessica had altered the room. The bed had been moved and the chest of drawers had been shifted. She stepped across the cat and opened Donny's side of the wardrobe and saw a line of empty hangers. She looked over at the boxes. Jessica was packing Donny away. On the landing were his music magazines. He'd collected them over the years and wouldn't throw them away even though Jessica was always moaning about them cluttering up the place. Now it looked as though everything was about to be moved out.

The spare room door was open and she peeked in. It was tidy but there were strange things dotted around. A huge rucksack was upright in the corner as well as a suitcase. There were some photographs on the top of the desk, of hills and mountains and people she didn't know. An unfamiliar towel hung on the radiator and some books were lined up on the bedside table with foreign sounding titles. On the bed was a throw with Aztec patterns on it.

She could hear voices from downstairs. It still sounded calm.

She went into her own room and put her bag down.

Jessica had been changing things in there as well. She'd taken the curtains down and put a roller-blind up. Something Lauren had wanted for a while. The brown desk where Lauren's computer had sat had gone and it was replaced by a bigger, newer desk with drawers and more space. In the alcove, in front of her bookshelves, sat a cardboard box big enough to hold a television set. It wasn't like the ones with Donny's stuff in them, it looked old, the corners of it battered and it had the words *THIS WAY UP* on it. There were streaks of dust on the top as though it had been wiped with a damp cloth.

The front door shut with a bang. She tensed and went over to the window. Donny was walking out to the car. Had Jessica thrown him out? She heard footsteps up the stairs.

'Are you OK?' Jessica said, standing at her door.

'What's happening?'

'Donny's not staying tonight. He's going to go over to Tony and Sheila's. They'll put him up.'

'Oh,' Lauren said. 'Does this mean you're turning him down?'

Jessica ignored the question and came across and gave her a hug.

'I'm so pleased to see you. I've been worried. I know you're a big grown up girl but still . . .'

'You look well.'

'I am well.'

Jessica looked vibrant. In just a couple of weeks her skin was glowing and she'd had her hair cut short and spiky. She was wearing a top that Lauren hadn't seen and cut off jeans with flip-flops. She was a bit too thin but there was something energetic and healthy about her. Lauren felt stodgy and pale in comparison. Maybe it was finally time to have her hair cut into some kind of style.

'What did Donny say to you?' Jessica said.

'That he wants you back. That it's over with the woman. And there was a miscarriage.'

'It's a lot for me to take in,' Jessica said. 'He's coming back tomorrow. I've said that we'll talk then.'

Lauren stared at her aunt. She couldn't work out what she was thinking.

'He can't just walk in here and pick up where he left off.'

'I know.'

'I'm happy now.'

'Are you and Zak? You know . . .'

'No! Zak's just an old friend. He's company. It's not even him that's cheered me up it's being back here. Among friends. I hated London.'

'It's not so bad . . .' Lauren said, thinking of Nathan and the dogs and Julie and Ryan.

'You look hot, why don't you get a shower? Then come downstairs. I'll get you some food and drink and we can talk. Zak'll be out all evening.'

Jessica turned to go then her eye rested on the cardboard box by the shelves.

'Oh, guess what? I was clearing stuff out of the loft when I came across your mum's doll's house. It was the one thing I kept from the house in London. I thought you could have it, you know, when you had your own family. I was going to have it renovated and give it to you as a present but then lately, when you were talking about your Art exam work I thought I'd give it to you now.'

'It's meant to be yours. Mum said it belonged to you and her.'

'I want you to have it.'

'If you're sure . . .' Lauren said, looking at the dog-eared box with much more interest.

'I don't know what sort of state it's in. The removal men packed it away and when we arrived here I told them to put it up in the loft. It hasn't seen the light of day since. Still, being an antique that might be a good thing. Anyway, have a shower and I'll open some wine. Pasta all right?'

Lauren nodded. Jessica walked out of the room.

'I was right, wasn't I?' she called after her.

'About what?' Jessica called from halfway down the stairs.

'I told you Donny would come back.'

There was no answer. Just the sound of footsteps getting further away.

# 26

By the time they'd eaten and washed up it was almost ten o'clock. They sat talking and Jessica drank several glasses of wine while Lauren stuck to water. Jessica was optimistic and gossipy, telling her all about things that had happened locally since they went away. All the while the kittens, much bigger now, played around at her feet while Cleopatra sat haughtily on the arm of a chair.

Jessica didn't mention Donny. After a while Lauren had to bring it up.

'I thought you'd be pleased about Donny.'

'I am.'

'I thought you still loved him.'

'I do but I need to take it slowly. I've just spent the last couple of months feeling like my insides have been kicked about. I have to be careful. He's feeling bruised because it's over with his girlfriend. That doesn't mean that he's ready to come back to me. Or that I'm ready to have him back.'

'He wants you to come back to London.'

'It's not going to happen. I came back here and felt immediately calmer, more like myself than I had been for months. This is where I belong. This is where my girls belong,' she said pulling one of the kittens away from the play fight it was having and folding it onto her lap. 'If Donny wants me he'll have to come back here.'

A ring-tone sounded. Jessica picked up her phone. She looked at the screen.

'Talk of the devil,' she said. 'Hi, Donny.'

She looked half annoyed and half pleased. She took her mobile out into the kitchen and Lauren sat back and tried to watch television. She was feeling tired. She couldn't help over hearing part of the conversation that was taking place beind her.

*I know . . . I know . . . I do understand . . . I'm not sure . . . I'm happy now . . . I don't want any more upheaval . . . I know you are . . . You don't have to keep saying that . . . It's not going to change anything. I know . . . I know.*

She went upstairs and looked for her own mobile. On the screen were two messages from Nathan. She read them and took a few moments to reply. An immediate beep came with an answer. *Miss you. I won't be able to sleep on my own.* The night before came back into her mind. She hadn't slept much with him then, she'd been in her parents' old bedroom, having a dream so vivid it seemed as though she'd seen it in a movie, that she could replay it if she wanted. She'd woken up in a state and he'd been there, in the room, ready to comfort her.

Nathan had been the one good thing to happen to her this summer.

So many other things had changed irrevocably. Her belief in Donny and Jessica as a couple. That had been the first big crack in her view of the world. Then there was the absolute certainty that she'd felt about the morning her mum and her sister died. That had been like concrete but it had begun to crumble at the edges as soon as the clown had come into her head. Rachel Morris had brought him to life, given him a name but she'd known about him before that. She'd pictured him on the first day that she'd seen the house. The theme for her Art exam had triggered her childhood memories or maybe it was seeing the house or both. The clown who had first brought a smile to her mum's face. Then he'd sent her into such a panic that she had tried to shut him out and brought Lauren into her bed so that they could all be safe together. Jessica and Donny had been in Spain. Her dad had moved in with his new girlfriend. Her mum had had no one to turn to.

Had her mum let William Doyle into her house that morning? Or the night before? Had they argued? Had he tried to kill the whole family? Why? Because her mum didn't like him? Didn't want to see him? Was afraid of him?

She felt herself getting anxious and paced up and down in the room. She'd done what she could. She'd sent all the information to Rachel Morris and now it was up to her to sort it out.

And then at some point she would have to tell Jessica all about it.

She went out onto the landing and listened. Jessica's voice was low and firm, still talking to Donny. If only she

225

could tell her *now*. Share it all with her, let her know what had been happening.

She went back into her room pushing down a feeling of frustration.

Her eye settled on the cardboard box. Her mum's doll's house. Like a visitor from the past. She'd thought about it over and over again in the last few months and here it was.

She turned to one of the drawers in the new desk and took out a pair of scissors. She pulled the point of the blade along the tape at the top and split it so that she could get her fingers in. Then she pulled at the cardboard until the top flaps came apart and were lying open.

A plasticky smell came out. When she looked she saw two inflated plastic bags that were lying across the top of the house. She pulled them out and saw the steeped roof and the chimney pots. She felt a flicker of anticipation. She was keen to see the house, the rooms and the figures. She wondered if the contents of the house had been packed separately. She tried to put her hands down the sides but there was more packing. She pulled out sheets of bubble wrap from all around it. When she'd got it all out she sat back. She looked at it with consternation. The house was big and would be too heavy for her to lift out by herself. Jessica was on the phone and in any case she didn't want to involve her aunt in this in case it brought back old memories and upsets.

The front door sounded then and she went out onto the landing.

'I'm back,' Zak called out for everyone to hear.

'Jessie's on the phone to Donny,' she said pointing towards the kitchen. 'I wondered if you could do me a favour?'

'Sure,' he said.

He came upstairs and followed her into her room. She could hear his wooden clogs clunking up each step. There was something else as well, another sound. When he came into the room she realised that he was humming a tune.

'It's this,' she said, pointing at the box. 'It's a doll's house. If I take two corners and you take two, we could lift it out.'

'Will do!' he said, helpfully.

Lauren put a hand under the drainpipe at the front of the house. Zak put his at the back.

'Easy does it,' he said, as it started to lift.

It was heavy, really heavy. It came a few inches and she could feel movement inside it as if the furniture was rattling around. She strained with her arms but all the weight was at the bottom of the house.

'Wait, I can't,' she said, her palms sore where the corners were sticking into them.

They lowered it back. Her shoulders dropped with disappointment.

'Wait a minute,' Zak said, looking as though he was thinking hard. 'Problem solving is my speciality.'

She waited feeling silly.

'I know,' he said. 'Got your scissors?'

She handed the scissors to him. He squatted down and began to cut down the side of the box. He cut a few inches and then took the cardboard in his hand and tore it away. A great bite of it came off and she could see the upper storey windows.

'If we peel the sides down then we can get a better grip of it.'

Zak continued peeling and cutting and she helped. He hummed as he did it, every now and then breaking into lyrics. In a few minutes a lot of the cardboard was lying on the floor.

'Now we should lift it,' he said.

She put her hands on the front of the house and let some of her fingers go through the windows as if they were handles.

'Ready?' he said.

She nodded.

'One, two, three!'

They lifted the house clear of the cardboard and set it on the floor.

'Is this where you want it?' he said.

She looked around the room. It would be better higher so that she could look into it, fix any furniture that had moved about.

'On my desk?' she said.

'Will do!' he said.

They lifted it together and carried it gingerly across and set it on the desk top.

'There!' Zak said, clapping his hands up and down.

Jessica appeared at the door and looked admiringly at the doll's house.

'That was quick,' she said. 'Careful, it might have splinters.'

'I don't think so,' Lauren said, looking in the windows, frowning because all the furniture and figures had moved into a pile in each room.

'It's a mess!' Jessica said.

'It should have been cleared out before it was packed up.'

'My fault,' Jessica said, 'I should have done it but I couldn't go back to the house again. I just let the removal men do it. At least it's still in one piece.'

'I'll sort it out,' Lauren said.

'Want a beer?' Zak said, looking at both of them.

Jessica nodded but Lauren shook her head and Zak went off.

'Thanks,' Lauren called.

'He's nice,' Jessica said. 'A bit strange looking but that's what two years in South America has done for him.'

'How's Donny?'

'Contrite.'

'And?'

'We'll see. I'm not rushing anything.'

'We both have to go back to London tomorrow.'

'There'll be other weekends,' Jessica said.

She nodded.

'Are you going to join us downstairs?'

Lauren shook her head. 'I'm really tired.'

'See you in the morning,' Jessica said, going out of the door. 'Then you can sort the doll's house out. You never know, it might be valuable. You could sell it and buy a car.'

Lauren sat down on the bed looking through the tiny windows to the jumble of people and furniture inside.

She knew she would never sell the doll's house.

# 27

She slept heavily. There were no dreams, just blackness, and when she woke she was surprised to see that it was still night even though she felt bright and alert as if she'd been asleep for ten hours. It was raining. She hadn't pulled the roller-blind down and saw the glass glistening with drops. It was chilly so she got up and closed the small window at the top. A car was coming up from the town, winding up the hill, its headlights tracing the bend in the road. The rain slanted determinedly through the beam of its lights. It was 2:19. As the car passed the house there was a burst of distant music, a heavy bass then it was gone and there were just two dots of red light disappearing up the hill. Maybe it was some young people making their way home after a late night in the town. Possibly she might have known them or maybe not. They could have been holidaymakers on their way back to some cottage or caravan park.

The road outside was silent. The only sound was the pitting of rain on the glass. She pulled the roller-blind down so that it covered the window.

She went to the bathroom and used the toilet. On the way back she glanced in at Jessica. She was fast asleep, her spiky hair standing upright from the pillow. She passed by Zak's room as quietly as she could and went downstairs. She got a glass of water and drank it down. Going back to her room she saw that the loft ladder had been put back up in the loft. She glanced at the piles of magazines in the plastic boxes and wondered whether they would have to be lifted back up into the loft and stored away again. Or would Donny squeeze them into the boot of his car and take them and his boxes of clothes back to London?

In her room she looked at the doll's house. Why not tidy it up now? She didn't feel sleepy. Why not do it there and then? She closed the door to her room and put the light on. She shivered a little so she pulled open her drawers and took out some old pyjama bottoms and a long sleeved cardigan. She put them on and sat down.

She would have to take everything out and maybe give it a dust before placing things back in. It made sense to do it room by room and she decided to start at the ground floor living room. She slipped a catch at the side and the front panel swung towards her like a door opening. She pulled it a hundred and ninety degrees and then hooked it back so that she could work on the interior of the house. It was a mess, furniture and figures flung about when it had been moved. The house itself had been buffeted but the contents had just fallen and tumbled, like dice in a pot.

She took everything out of the living room and lined the pieces up on the side. She was surprised to see that there was a carpet on the floor, a circular rug with a border of patterns. She held it up. It was the size of a saucer. She got some tissues and dusted around and then replaced the rug and the chairs and the figures. There were three small paintings and a mirror that had sat over the fireplace. She wondered how to put them back and then she used her fingers to feel around the walls. A splinter of loose wood pricked her and she pulled her hand out, put the finger in her mouth and sucked it. Then, gingerly she reached in again and found a tiny tack on each wall. She got the pictures and with some difficulty managed to fix them back on the wall. Then she did the same with the mirror.

The first room was done. Looking at the entire house it seemed odd. One ordered room and chaos elsewhere.

There was some noise from the next room. It sounded like Jessica turning over in her bed. Had she made a noise and woken her? Lauren went quickly out into the hall and peeked into the room next door. Jessica had pulled the duvet up over her head and was completely still.

Back in her room Lauren started on the kitchen of the house.

She held the figure of a woman in her hand. Her legs were straight and stiff as was the rest of her. Not like modern toy figures which moved so that they could be repositioned if necessary. She was dressed in grey, a servant. She laid the figure on her desk surface and continued removing the jumble of pots and pans from the mess. She took everything out, marvelling at the number of small items, plates and dishes and even a colander and a rolling pin. She righted the French dresser up against the wall and moved the big kitchen table back to the centre of the room. She replaced the rest and looked critically at it.

She had never been allowed to do anything like this when she was a child. Five minutes or so was the most she had ever been allowed to play with it. Except for those early mornings when she woke up and sat down in front of it making up stories about the people inside. And yet her mum had tried to get Jessica interested in it by making up little games. Jessica, who hated it, could have played with it all she wanted but Lauren wasn't allowed.

The rain was hammering down against the glass outside. She pulled her cardigan around her and thought about pulling on a pair of socks.

Before she started on the child's bedroom she noticed something odd. There was a pen lying up against the wall. A proper pen, not a toy one. She took it out. It looked surreal. She began to remove things. The tiny bed was on top of the figures and toys which made a heap in the middle of the room. She picked out the figure of a boy, his cheeks plump and reddened. She took out the wardrobe and chest of drawers which were intact but she saw, with dismay, that some of the more fragile pieces were broken. The rocking chair looked as though one of its rockers had snapped off and it just fell forward when she tried to stand it up. A toy pram had lost most of its handle and the legs of a highchair had snapped.

If she could find the small pieces of wood she could repair them. There were lots of bits still strewn about but really she needed better light to see in and find the tiny bits of wood. If she felt about she might end up with another splinter.

She went downstairs, her feet hardly touching each step and got a torch from the kitchen drawer. Back in her room she shone the torch into the bedroom. There were a number of pieces of wood and she picked each one out and lined it up on the desk surface to look at later. The curved piece was the first that she matched up and she felt herself smile. It would be possible to fix it. She turned back to the almost empty room. The floor had a carpet. It wasn't fitted but it covered most of the space. There were still some scrappy bits of toys on it and a couple of pictures that had fallen off the walls. She decided to pull it out so that the broken pieces came with it. She tugged it gently and saw it come towards her.

Something caught her eye.

A wad of paper underneath the carpet. White paper.

She frowned. The paper was unnaturally bright amid the browns and greens and yellows of the house. She wondered if it had been put there to line the carpet. She put the torch down and pulled the carpet with both hands taking care not to scatter any of the broken bits on top of it. Letting go of one edge she plucked the paper out and tossed it to the side. Then she continued pulling and cupped the carpet with both hands underneath and transferred it onto the desk.

Her hands were dusty and she rubbed them on her cardigan. She looked around. On the desk was a line of pieces and a few broken items. She found herself licking her lips. She wished she had a glass of water. She stretched her arms and looked at the paper. Why had that been put in there she wondered. She picked it up. It was just some sheets of A4 folded in four. She put it down and looked again at the carpet. Possibly it was a bit more threadbare than the rug in the living room or maybe the flooring in the bedroom wasn't so solid. She shone the torch onto the floor of the room. It looked flat and firm.

She turned the torch off. Then she pulled the paper towards her and began to unfold it. As she did she saw something she hadn't noticed before. On the inside of the fold was a word. She read it and felt her breath catch in her throat.

*Jessica.*

She unfolded the sheets completely so that she was able to flatten them. The desk had no space though, the doll's house and the pieces that she'd taken out had filled up the surface. She turned to her bed and flatted the sheets out on her duvet.

There were three sheets of paper covered in small handwriting. All written in pen. At the top it said, *My dear, dear, Jessica.* She glanced down the first page. Some of the paragraphs were at a slant. Some had darker writing and in places it got more faint. On the second page the writing seemed to get smaller and then bigger and waver across the page. There was even some words written up the side as if by afterthought. The third page was only three quarters full and at the very end after a line of large writing that said *I love you I love you I love you* was the word

GRACE

It was a letter from her mother to her aunt.

Lauren left the paper on her duvet and walked across the room as if to distance herself from it. Her mother's words. Her voice from the past, from ten years ago. She held her breath for a long time. She knew that this was something important, something momentous.

The doll's house sat silently, its rooms shadowy, only half fixed. Around it were bits and pieces from inside, some of them broken, casualties of the move. Her mother's letter had sat inside it for ten years, her voice smothered by a square of carpet.

Lauren walked back to the bed and with trembling fingers she picked it up.

# 28

The letter was hard to read. The handwriting was erratic and small, in places tiny. The pen seemed to fade in parts as if the words had gone soft or been whispered. In some cases part of a word had disappeared and been written over more heavily. The punctuation was sometimes there, sometimes not and at times it was overdone.

But it was from her mother. And she read it slowly, scrutinising the words. She felt as though she was decoding something. The first page took the longest because she had to go over parts again.

*My dear, dear Jessica What will you think when you get this letter? You will think I have gone completely mad and maybe you will be right. I am mad in a way, I'm not bad. You will find this and read about me and no doubt you will wonder what happened to your poor sad sister when you went to Spain. Who would have thought that I could ever be with another man after Robbie????? I met him a couple of weeks ago at a neighbour's party. He was the party entertainer and he was dressed up as a clown. He was very funny but that was just a mask, underneath was nasty nasty .You wouldn't believe the filth that I found under that mask. I didn't start seeing him then, oh no, it was a few days later when I bumped into him a shop. He gave me his card because I said I might have a party for Lauren when it was her birthday. I rang him. Billy, his name was. He wasn't much to look at but he had such a friendly face and he said he loved children, he just loved working with them, he just made them laugh, he had a way with them. I couldn't see through it. I believed him. It's hard when you've been dumped by your husband, left with two kids, who will want you??? Who will want to take on two kids and a rejected woman? Not many men, but he did. He was nice and funny and I liked the fact that he wasn't good-looking (Robbie was good-looking and look where that got me). I thought it might be the start of something. He was so good with Daisy, he held her and sang to her but this makes me feel sick when I think about my sweet baby being held by that animal. He liked Lauren as well, but he said he wasn't going to rush things, older kids take their time to get to know you and you can't rush it and like a fool I believed him, I believed him, what an idiot I was, what a total moron I was!!!! I couldn't see through his lies to the creature that was underneath. Oh no.*

Lauren had to stop reading. It was as if her mother's voice was pouring this anguish into her ear. William Doyle *had* been seeing her mum. The thought of it made her feel sick. She knew now, ten years later, that he had killed other women and their children. But her mum couldn't have known that at the time of writing this letter. However afraid she had been she hadn't known what he was capable of.

A creak from the next room disturbed her. It was Jessica getting up out of bed. She knew the sound well enough. Her door opened and she heard her pad across to the bathroom. Moments later the toilet flushed and she heard her go back to her bed.

This was Jessica's letter. It had never been meant for her eyes. She held the pages to her chest for a moment wondering whether to go in and tell what she'd found. But Jessica might just shove it away somewhere. She might refuse to read it in the way that she refused to talk about the past. Worse, she might not even tell Lauren what was in it. She couldn't trust Jessica with this letter even though it was addressed to her. She had to read it so that she would know what to tell Rachel Morris about her mum and William Doyle.

She thought of her dad, Robbie, stuck in a prison cell. She hadn't set eyes on him or spoken to him for ten years. It was her evidence, recorded by video, that had put him behind bars.

She picked the letter up again. A line at the beginning of the second page had been completely crossed out. Lauren tried to read under the scribble but she couldn't.

*He came round to the house three days running. I thought he was keen. The first time the baby and Lauren were here. He was full of stories about the parties he had done and he did little tricks for Lauren that she liked. The second day I made him something to eat. He brought flowers and the funny thing was that he never tried to touch me, it was always just a kiss on the cheek and a hug. It was as if we were friends but honestly Jessie I didn't want a friend like him. The third day, a week ago Lauren was out at Molly's playing with the twins and Daisy was asleep. He brought a toy for Lauren* and I don't know why but I said he couldn't give it to her, what I meant was it was better to save it for a special occasion, it's not good for children to just get gifts for nothing and he was really upset about it and he left. I wasn't to know why he liked giving children gifts, how could I know that????? I thought about it, he was just being kind I thought, and I'd stamped all over his generosity. I misunderstood but that's me, I can never read between the lines I'm not that bright (Robbie knew it, that's why he was able to deceive me for so long, I always took things at face value) I was rubbish at understanding what was going on. I was desperate to see him and put things right. I tried calling him on his mobile but he never answered. Then last weekend when the children were asleep I did a bad thing. I left them alone and went out to his flat. It was only a few streets away. I just wanted to knock on the door and say sorry. Ask him if we could still be friends. He was in. If he hadn't been I would never have known what a monster he was. He seemed pleased to see me. He made me a cup of tea and said that he was the one who should be sorry. I finished my tea and I put my cup in the kitchen and I thought I'd better go back to the children and I turned to go and saw this open door. It was the door to his bedroom and I was puzzled by some pictures that were stuck on the wall so I went closer and gave the door a push. The sight was horrible. The whole wall was covered in pictures of children, many of them cut out from magazines, the kind of pictures you get in catalogues when you're buying children's clothes. Many of them had only underwear on, it made me sick to my stomach, and all of a sudden it was as if the darkness had been lit up and I could see everything about this man. I ran past him out of the door and got home. I locked the door and sat on the floor, my heart pounding pounding pounding like it was

241

*going to burst out of my chest. I ran upstairs and my Lauren was fast asleep and so was my Daisy, my beautiful babies both of them so sweet, so innocent in this sick world, my poor sweet babies like flowers on a rubbish dump.*

Lauren put the second page down. Her mouth was dry and her back was stiff and she looked over at the doll's house. Her mum had left this letter there for Jessica to find. She had hidden it just as she had done when Jessica was a child. But Jessica had never found the letter because she had never touched the doll's house again. Removal men had packed it away and it had sat in their loft for ten years untouched, her mum's words unread.

William Doyle, the man who had killed her mother and her sister was free to go and do it again.

And her dad was innocent.

A feeling of hopelessness took hold of her. How could this have happened?

She looked at the last page.

*He came round to the house, knocking on the door. He wanted to explain, he said I'd got it all wrong, he said the pictures had been put up by another man who used to use that room but had moved out, but that was a lie. I might be stupid but I finally saw through him. I understood why he was so interested in me. How could it be for anything else? Why would anyone be interested in me? Look at me? No one no one no one has ever shown any interest in me, not even my husband. He phoned, he came round looking in the window. I told him to go away, I told him to leave me alone, I said I'd go to the police, but he said if I did that they might think I was involved in something. The police work like that. One sniff of anything to do with children and the children get taken into care and he said I might never see them again. I didn't know what to do I couldn't go to the police. Today I was in the park and I saw him. He was sitting on a bench reading a newspaper. The bench was next to the children's play area. I watched him talking to some boys and I panicked and rushed away but he saw me and came after me so I ran and ran and ran down the street until we got home and I put the bolt on the door. I'm afraid he will not leave me alone or my girls. Oh yes he will come back. This world is a terrible place Jessica. I can't go on in it. I can't be in it any more and I can't leave my children behind me. Who would protect them? Their father??????? Oh no, no, no I can't trust him. Even if I could there are other evil people like Billy who will ferret them out, find them at parties and suck them down into darkness. I can't let that happen to my children. I can't I can't I can't. I love them too much. Don't hate me, Jessica. I love you and I love them. You're all grown now but they're not and I can't protect them. Look at what I did. I nearly brought that vile man into their lives. It was my fault. I offered my children on a plate. This is no world for me to live and I won't leave them behind. I won't hurt them. I'll wait until they're asleep. I wouldn't hurt them for the world. I love you I love you I Love you Grace*

Lauren felt very cold. She pulled her cardigan around her tightly. Inside she felt hollow. There was a great deep dark space in her chest. Her jaw began to tremble and when she put her fingers up to her eyes they were wet and hot.

'Oh Mum,' she said. 'Oh Mum.'

She turned the paper over. She picked up the other sheets and looked searchingly at them. That couldn't be all there was. There must be more. There had to be more. She got off the bed and went across to the doll's house. She looked in the room again, then into the last room, the one she hadn't cleared. It was the parents' bedroom. It was a mess as the other rooms had been. She put her hand in and pulled the things out. It only took a second to empty it, the beds, the wardrobes, the carpets spilled out, fell onto the floor or the chair. There had to be another piece of paper, another letter, another explanation. When the room was empty she went back to the others, the ones she had already tidied up, and swept them clear tipping away the furniture and figures she had previously worked on.

All the rooms were empty.

There had to be another page, hidden somewhere.

She put her arms around the entire structure and tipped it towards her. It was heavy but she shook it hoping that something would fall out from a hiding place.

Wasn't that what her mum did? Hide letters for Jessica to find? Now it was Lauren who would find it. Nothing moved though so she tipped it to one side and shook it harder, making a banging sound on the desk.

Lauren who was meant to be dead. Killed by her father.

Her bedroom door swung open. It was Jessica looking sleepy and puzzled.

'What are you doing? It's three o'clock in the morning! What's going on?'

Nothing was coming out of the house. She should turn it upside down.

'What's the matter? Why is it such a mess in here? What are you doing?'

With a huge effort she pulled the doll's house over making a loud bang. It laid on its front, its open side down on the desk. Her mum must have slipped something in between the walls. She needed to break into them. She felt Jessica's hands on her arms as she gave an almighty push and the doll's house toppled off the desk onto the floor. It rocked for a moment and settled on its side.

'Lauren stop it! STOP IT! STOP IT!'

She shook off Jessica's arms and picked up the torch. Using it like a hammer she started to hit the side of the doll's house. If she had to demolish it she would. She would smash it up in order to find what she was looking for. Hidden pages from her mum. She would find them.

She hit the wood four, five, six times and then she stopped and felt herself go limp, the torch hanging in her hand. She looked at Jessica who was standing with her mouth open, an expression of shock on her face.

There were no more pages.

Behind Jessica she could see Zak, a concerned look on his face.

'Everything all right?'

'No, it's not,' she said.

'It's OK Zak, I'll deal with this,' Jessica said.

Zak shrugged and backed away. Jessica closed the room door.

'What's the matter, Lolly?' she whispered coming forward, her arms out. 'What's happened to you?'

Lauren pointed to the bed.

'It's a letter for you. From my mum,' she said.

# 29

Jessica read the pages standing up. She had a sleeveless T-shirt on over her pants. Her hair was standing bolt upright at the front. Her legs were thin her knees bony. She looked cold, her skin had goosepimples. Lauren put her hand onto Jessica's arm but Jessica shook it off and turned away as if she didn't want anyone to touch her. Jessica's eyes travelled from one side of the page to the other. She didn't look up, she didn't stop reading. She turned the page quickly creasing it putting the top one back in the wrong order, at the wrong angle. Lauren wanted to take it from her, square it up, tidy the pages.

'I don't believe it,' she said, when she got to the end, 'I don't believe it. Grace would never . . .'

Then she slumped onto the bed and started to read it again peering at the words as though the whole thing had been written in Russian.

The doll's house lay on the floor of Lauren's room damaged, a hole in its side and a corner of the roof collapsed. The panel which comprised the front of the house had broken off and lay half under it. The figures and pieces were strewn around. It was just a pile of broken toys. Lauren made a half-hearted attempt to clear it up. From behind she heard Jessica's voice.

'Leave it.'

She looked round and Jessica had her hands over her mouth. There was a choking sound coming from her and she was shaking her head from side to side. Lauren stepped across and hugged her aunt. She put both arms around her and pulled her close. She could feel the bones in her shoulders and her elbows.

A purring sound came from the door and she could see Cleopatra standing peeking into the room.

'I don't understand. How could this be?' Jessica said.

Lauren took the pages from her and put them on the side table. Outside the rain had lessened. She could just hear it pattering against the glass. Jessica started to shiver.

'Lie down,' she said, pulling her aunt to the side, scrabbling about with the duvet finding the right edge of it to pull up over the two of them. 'Try and sleep.'

But they didn't sleep. Lauren lay with her arm around Jessica and stared into the room as the daylight seeped in around the edges of the new roller-blind.

At a little after five Jessica sat up.

'I need to talk to Donny,' she said, her voice croaky.

'Wait,' Lauren said. 'Before you do there's some other stuff. Things that have happened in London that I didn't tell you about. Things about my dad . . . And about the old house.'

'I don't think I can take any more surprises.'

'Before you call Donny. You need to hear it all.'

There was movement from the spare room. The floorboards were creaking.

'That's Zak,' Jessica said. 'He goes walking every Sunday. Wait till he goes. Then we'll get up and you can tell me what's been happening in London.'

Lauren nodded.

'Then I'll call Donny.'

Donny came just after nine. Lauren opened the door and felt the chill wind. Outside the sky was flat and grey and the street was wet, the hedges glistening.

'What's up, Lolly?' he said.

He was rubbing his hands together. He had a T-shirt and jeans on but looked cold. Jessica was standing in the kitchen. She'd put on jogging trousers and a jumper. Her hair was flat where she'd wet it. Her skin looked grey and washed out.

'What's happened?' he said, looking worried.

Jessica pointed to the letter on the table.

'What's this?' he said.

'It's from my sister,' she said. 'Read it.'

Later, Donny hugged a mug of tea.

'Poor Grace,' he said. 'Poor lady. I had no idea she was capable of something like that.'

The letter lay on the table between them. It had been read and re-read by each of them.

'We have to go back to London,' Jessica said.

Donny nodded.

'I'll pack some stuff. I can be ready in half an hour.'

Jessica was washing cups and plates. She had her back to him. Lauren watched as Donny stood up and stepped across to her. He put his arms around her. Lauren could sense her stopping what she was doing. After a couple of seconds she turned and put her face in Donny's chest. Her hands were covered in soap suds and she held them up away from Donny's clothes.

'Poor Grace,' she said. 'My poor Grace.'

Lauren felt her eyes glassing over again. She walked out of the room and the words *What about my dad?* went through her head but she didn't say them.

They left for London just before ten. Lauren was in the front passenger seat and Donny was driving. Jessica was in the back. Beside her, on the seat, was a small overnight bag. The road was half empty. There were few lorries and hardly any cars. It took them an hour and a half to get to Exeter and then they were on the motorway. There was no music on in the car, just the low voice of a twenty-four hour news station. None of them said much. Jessica fell asleep for a while, her face up against the window. Lauren sent a long text to Nathan. She didn't go into details she just said that some things had been sorted out and that she would tell him later.

They stopped near Bath for petrol. Then they continued on until they were just outside London. Donny pulled in at the services.

'I need a break,' he said. 'I'll get some coffee. Anyone want some?'

Jessica nodded and Lauren shook her head. When Donny walked away Jessica leaned forward and rubbed Lauren's arm up and down.

'Are you all right?' she said.

Lauren nodded.

'This is the right thing to do. Get back to London. See the solicitor.'

'I know.'

'Your mum was sick, Lauren. That's what you have to remember. She wasn't in her right mind.'

'I know.'

'She was desperately sick and no one knew.'

Jessica's voice dropped to a whisper as if she was just talking to herself. When Donny got back to the car he handed Jessica her coffee and then stood by the driver's door drinking from his cup.

'I don't forgive your father, though,' Jessica said.

Lauren frowned.

'I know you don't want to hear this but I'll say it just once and never again. If he had treated her better, looked after her, cared for her, *loved* her she would have been a different person.'

Lauren shook her head. She didn't want to think about it.

'Maybe that's why he didn't love her?' Donny said, leaning into the car, 'Because she was the way she was. You can't put everything at his door, Jessie. Not now.

Not after ten years in a prison cell for something he didn't do.'

'He could have stopped it. If he had been a decent man . . .'

Lauren closed her eyes. She listened to the cars and lorries on the motorway. It was an uninterrupted drone of traffic which drowned out much of what they were saying.

'He's an innocent man, Jessie.'

'He didn't do this! But he did other things.'

'Grace killed Daisy. She tried to kill Lolly. She's not completely innocent!'

My sister was ill . . . She was ill . . .'

'Stop, stop, STOP IT!'

Lauren was crying. They both stared at her. Donny got into the car and Jessica leaned forward and gripped her shoulder.

'This isn't the time to talk about it all,' Jessica said, her voice calm.

'There'll be a lot of time to sort it all out. When we get back to London. Plenty of time,' Donny said.

There was a hint of satisfaction in Donny's words. He was bringing Jessica and Lauren back to London, to the house in Bethnal Green, as he had said he would. The circumstances were different than what he might have hoped. Lauren watched him put the car in gear and drive out of the service station. He was stony-faced but she sensed that underneath that there was some pleasure of a sort. He was in charge. He was looking after them.

When they came off the motorway and made their

way through central London Lauren began to feel apprehension. When she saw the sign for *Bethnal Green* she felt a growing ache in her chest. *49, Hazelwood Road, Bethnal Green.* She had been there and conquered her fears but that was before she knew the truth of what happened.

'There's somewhere I want you to take me,' she said. 'I want all three of us to go. Please.'

She didn't look into the back seat to see Jessica's expression. She imagined her aunt stiffening up.

'It won't take long but I have to go there. And I want you both to come with me.'

'Where?' Donny said, glancing sideways at her, looking puzzled.

'I know where she wants to go,' Jessica said.


They drove up to 49 Hazelwood Road. Donny parked the car a few houses along. They got out and walked towards the front of the house. Seconds later Nathan came out. He walked straight up to Lauren and hugged her.

'This is Jess,' Lauren said, pointing. 'And this is Donny.' Nathan nodded at them.

'This, obviously, is Nathan.'

'Are you sure your parents won't mind us coming in?' Jessica said, briskly, as if she wanted to get it over with.

'No, they won't mind. Not at all.'

The dogs greeted them in the hallway as Jessica and Donny walked through into the back kitchen. Donny sat down on a chair and started to pat the dogs.

'I love these dogs. Retrievers? Lovely. I've always wanted a dog.'

'They're a bit mad sometimes and they need a lot of exercise.'

'That'd suit me. I've put on a bit of weight.'

Jessica didn't sit down. She was looking around the kitchen. Then she stood at the window and looked out.

'Your parents have certainly changed things,' she said.

Lauren took her arm, 'I want you to come upstairs with me.'

Jessica shook her head.

'I need to say goodbye. Now that I know what really happened. You need to do it as well.'

'Do you want me to come?' Donny said, one of his hands stroking the length of Prince's back.

Lauren shook her head. She pulled at Jessica's arm. Jessica started to move. They walked along the hallway and up the stairs. The door to her mother's old bedroom was closed and she turned the handle and went in, pulling Jessica with her.

'It's just a room now,' she said.

Jessica looked stricken.

'I was here,' Lauren said. 'Daisy was there and Mum was over there.'

They both looked at the place where Lauren was pointing.

'Poor Grace,' Jessica said.

An image of her dad came into Lauren's head. She couldn't be sure that it was his face any more because it was so long since she had seen him. It was a man with a bewildered look on his face. In his hand was a knife.

She took a deep breath.

'Let's go,' she said, taking Jessica's hand again.

# 30

Lauren was sitting in the café at the Museum of Childhood. Nathan was beside her. Opposite was Julie Bell and Ryan Lassiter. Around the outside of the café area were groups of school children milling about, some holding hands, waiting in line, doing what they were told. Others had broken free and were running up and down the lines. Harassed adults were trying to keep them together.

'What a din!' Julie said.

The collective noise of the children was loud. There were waves of chatter, ripples of laughter and occasional screeches that reminded Lauren of the seagulls at St Agnes, demanding and raucous.

'So,' Julie said, turning back towards Nathan and Lauren. 'It turns out that Ryan's considering applying to Nottingham as well. What a coincidence! We can both be freshers together.'

'Nottingham,' Ryan confirmed.

Lauren smiled. There wasn't a centimetre between Julie and Ryan, his brown forearm making her white skin look even paler today than normal. Strangely Julie was dressed less flamboyantly than usual. She had on a dark blue blouse and jeans and a blue Alice band in her hair. Her lipstick was light pink, hardly noticeable. Even more strangely, Ryan was wearing an oversized white T-shirt and skinny jeans and plimsolls. It was nothing like his usual outfit.

'All right, Nath!' a voice boomed from behind.

They turned round. It was a young lad wearing the café uniform.

'Hi, Tom, how's the job going?' Nathan said, standing up.

'It's all right. Manager's a bit of a pain,' he said, lowering his voice, eyeing a woman behind the counter.

'She's all right when you get to know her. Ask her about her horses. She loves talking about them.'

Lauren turned back to Julie and Ryan as Nathan talked on.

'When is your dad going to be released?' Julie said.

'His appeal is fixed for September fourth. That date still stands. But he's been given bail pending the trial. It means he should be out of prison by the end of July.'

'I still can't believe it. When you told me what had happened I just thought, *She's having me on!* I said that to Ryan. Didn't I?'

'She did,' Ryan confirmed.

It was a week since she'd told Julie. Her friend had sat open mouthed in the college refectory as she'd explained it all. She'd twiddled with a long fringy scarf winding it around her wrist and undoing it again. She hadn't needed to tell her but she'd wanted to. Julie had been a good friend and she didn't want her to find out about it from the press after she'd gone back to Cornwall.

'Are you going to see your dad? To meet him when he comes out? At the prison gates? It'd be like a movie.'

She shook her head. 'I'll be three hundred miles away in St Agnes.'

'Don't you want to see him? After all this time?'

'I do but it's not the right time. There's legal stuff going on and the press will be around. I don't want to get drawn into all that.'

'See you, mate,' Nathan said, sitting back down.

She turned and watched as the lad walked back towards the counter where a stony-faced woman was waiting for him.

Nathan put his hand on her arm. He had his *Cuba* T-shirt on. It reminded her of that first day she'd met him months before when she'd gone to the house in Hazelwood Road. That single act, bumping into him, had changed everything. Or maybe it was her returning to the house, like a ghost from the past, that had started it all off.

Now she was leaving London to go back to St Agnes and live with Jessica. She would finish her 'A' levels at Perranporth. She would decide which uni to apply for. Life would go back to the way it had been before they moved to London. Except that everything in her life now was different. She knew the truth about her family. That knowledge had calmed her, made her feel more in control.

'I'll get some more drinks,' Nathan said, standing up.

'I'll come with you,' Ryan said.

When they'd gone Julie grabbed her hand.

'Are you really all right? You've been through the most terrible time. Ryan says that people never get over the kind of shocks that you've had.'

'I'm all right,' Lauren said, 'Really.'

The previous weekend she and Donny had gone to visit the grave. They'd walked along together, through the uneven pathways of the cemetery. A warm breeze was blowing into their faces. Donny had been in his work suit and had had to undo his tie. After a few minutes he took his jacket off as well.

The grave was well kept and tidy. Jessica had arranged payment and it had been cared for by the cemetery for ten years. Since the funeral it hadn't been a place that they visited. Even when they moved back to London they hadn't come. Until now.

Donny laid a bunch of pink carnations on the flat stone and Lauren squatted down to look at the two oval photographs on the headstone. After so long the pictures must have faded in colour she was sure. Her mum was smiling but Daisy looked sleepy. Underneath were the words. *At rest, Grace, beloved mother and Daisy beloved sister.* The words made her throat fill up for a second.

She'd tried to feel anger towards her mum but it wouldn't come. She'd gone through some old photos that Jessica had given her and looked closely at her mum's face. The only emotion she felt was a deep longing to see her again, to go back in time and look after her, to stop what had happened, but it wasn't possible. She only felt sad.

The cemetery was quiet. In the distance she could hear the traffic but it was muted as if this place was somehow sealed off from the rest of the town. The nearby trees rippled in the breeze, the flowers on the graves dropped their petals, butterflies fluttered around the bushes. Only the gravestones were utterly still.

'You saying a prayer, Lolly?' Donny said.

Lauren shook her head.

'What about your uncle,' Julie said. 'Is he going back to Cornwall?'

'No, he has to stay in London until Christmas. The school want him to work out his notice.'

'Then what? Are they getting back together?'

'Maybe. Maybe not. Him and Jess are trying to work it out. I'm not exactly sure that she wants him back.'

Nathan came across with the drinks.

Jessica had been withdrawn ever since she'd read the letter. After seeing the solicitor she'd wanted to go straight back down to Cornwall. She wouldn't even stay one night in the house at Bethnal Green. Lauren went to Victoria Station with her. Jessica tried to explain, *Knowing what I know now it's as if it's only just happened. As if my sister died just before I read that letter. It's all fresh again, the grief. I can't believe it. It's ten years, I thought it was all over.*

Her emails since then were short and wooden. Her phone calls were full of long silences. She needed to get back to St Agnes to look after her.

'So, Nath, when do you go to Exeter?' Julie said.

'Not until the end of September,' he said. 'But I'm going down to Lauren's for a couple of weeks.'

'You'll be a beach bum,' Julie said.

'You could learn how to surf,' Ryan said, brightening up.

Julie put her arm around Ryan's shoulder and gave him a big, loud kiss on the cheek. She was smiling, as if he'd made a joke.

'Next summer me and Ryan will come down. How about that?'

'The waters are deep though. And dangerous,' Lauren said.

'And full of mermaids,' Nathan said.

'You know what they say about mermaids?'

'Mortals should stay away from them,' Nathan said, taking hold of a curl at the end of Lauren's hair and twisting it round his finger.

'They're talking in code,' Julie said in a fake whisper.

'Let's go,' Ryan said. 'Leave them on their own.'

On the way out of the museum Lauren stopped in the entrance and looked round at the giant doll's house. *Amy Miles' House 1890*. She stood in front of it and wondered if she would *feel* anything. She looked at the bedroom with its fireplace and pictures on the wall and on the wash stand a tiny bowl and jug. There would be no letter underneath that rug, no message from the past. The rest of the house was neat and tidy and grand, unlike her doll's house which was empty and broken, the furniture and fittings stored in a plastic box. Zak had said he was going to fix it but she didn't know whether she would ever want it again.

'Coming?' Nathan said.

She walked away, pulling her hair back with a tie.

# 31

*Dear Dad,*

*Your solicitor phoned me to say that you have won your appeal. I'm very glad for you. You must be relieved to have it all over and done with.*

*I'm sending this letter to Nana Jo and Granddad Ray because she says that you are going to live with them for a while in Northumberland.*

*I am still in St Agnes with Jessie. Donny is living in London and he comes down every other weekend. You probably don't know that they broke up earlier in the year but I've got my fingers crossed that they will get back together. My course at college starts in a couple of weeks and I'll be finishing my 'A' levels and applying for uni. I think I'm going to do some kind of art course. I've looked at the Exeter prospectus and I'm hoping to go there if I get the right grades.*

*I'm sorry I didn't reply to the letters you sent me through the summer. It's been a funny time for me. Jessie has been unwell and I've been looking after her. The whole thing was a huge shock for her. Of course it's been terrible for you too, I understand that. I know you've said that it wasn't my fault but I can't help feeling responsible for the fact that you spent ten years in prison. I don't know if I'll* ever be able to get past that. For all that time I've had these powerful feelings inside me. Grief and rage. It's hard for me to change those feelings overnight.

But I will try. I promise I will.

Thank you for the photo. You say that you've grown old in ten years but I don't think so. You've definitely got less hair but that's the only difference.

I'm sending a photo of me with this letter. Donny took it last weekend on the beach at St Agnes. The wind was blowing a gale that's why my hair is all over the place.

The solicitor told me that you wanted to meet me as soon as possible. I understand that. But do you mind if we take it slowly? Could we email each other for a while? I know you said, in one of your letters, that you'd been learning about computers. Could you get email? Then we could communicate with each other often.

I'd feel awkward coming up to Nana and Granddad's. If we are going to meet would you mind if we did it somewhere halfway? London maybe? Half term is at the end of October. Maybe that would be a good time. I could stay with Donny.

The solicitor also said that your asthma had been bad. You should definitely get a hospital appointment. There are masses of drugs they can give you for asthma.

My email address is at the bottom of this letter. I look forward to getting a message from you.

See you soon,

Love Lauren.

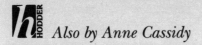 

**INNOCENT**

Charlie is well acquainted with the police. Her brother Brad is constantly in trouble. But this time it's serious. A man is dead and Brad is in the frame for his murder. Something about the crime doesn't add up, though. Charlie is convinced Brad is hiding something – or someone.

But in trying to prove her brother's innocence, is Charlie letting go of her own.